The Dim-Witted Hitman

Deb Graham

The Dim-Witted Hitman

© 2018 Deb Graham

Cover Design by Angelica Hagman

Other Books you may enjoy by Deb Graham:

Peril In Paradise   (a cruise novel)

Alaska Cruise with the Cruise Addict's Wife

and check out the other Cruise Addict's Wife books!

Complete list at end of this book

The Dim-Witted Hitman

Chapter one

Dimmie sipped his hot cocoa as his world crashed around him. His hand shook. With only hours left to live, he had blocked out Mam's voice in his mind about no sweets before dinner and asked for two donuts from the coffee bar. Extra whipped cream in the cocoa, too. He bit the jelly one first, wondering if being dead would hurt. He hadn't thought about if the people he'd killed felt any pain; he was just following orders. Last time the dentist had to fill a cavity, she had promised it wouldn't hurt, but it did. Would dying hurt as much as Dr Sim's drill? He'd find out soon enough. As soon as word reached the city about the mess he'd made, it'd be all over.

four days previous

The day started out like always, except the Boss called a meeting real early, even before Dimmie had a chance to eat his Pop-Tart for breakfast. The Boss must have something on his mind, but it didn't matter. Dimmie's job description was clear. So long as no one put out a hit on anybody, he really had nothing to do. He still had to show up when the crew met. Big Boss made that rule, and Little

Boss stuck to it. Old man Kerrick always said he wanted the younger boys to learn the ropes. Dimmie had no idea what the new boss wanted. After six years, the boys still didn't know what to expect half the time.

Dimmie half-listened as Lucky Callahan stormed around the room, keeping an eye on him in case anything was thrown his way. Lucky had a bee in his bustle, that was for sure. Dimmie wasn't sure what a bustle was, and there weren't many bees in the city, but Gran always said that when someone was upset, and Lucky Callahan was that this morning. Dimmie suppressed a yawn and picked at a dab of mud on his wet shoes. Rain: a wet day with a too-early start. He hoped his mother hadn't made up his bed before he went back home. He wanted a nap, but Mam would get after him if he dared mess up a neatly made bed. And how could a man sleep on top of the covers?

Brody elbowed Dimmie with a sharp hiss. Dimmie slammed his chair forward, all four chair legs on the floor. Mam always told him not to rear back on two legs so he didn't fall backward, but he'd never fallen backward. And anyway, he liked it. Perspiration broke out on his brow. Why had Brody elbowed him?

He tended to be forgotten in these meetings unless Lucky wanted somebody rubbed out. He realized he'd missed whatever Lucky had said. *Wool-gathering,* Gran would sniff, but Gran never came to these meetings. Women didn't know about the mob, or they acted like it, at least. Men's work. Everybody knew that.

"Dimmie, my boy, it looks like you're going on a luxury cruise."

Dimmie blinked, his jaw slack. He knew all those words, but not in that order. A luxury cruise? Living with Mam and Gran above the shop, *luxury* was a word applied to other people, not the O'Malleys. And going? What did Little Boss mean, *going?* Dimmie didn't go anywhere; he'd hardly ever been out of the five boroughs. He liked it that way. Mam kept the television on day and night, and he saw what people outside the city were like. No, he never went anywhere.

Dimmie shook his head to clear it. "What's that, Little Bo—I mean, Lucky? Me?"

"Yes, you." His mind made up, Lucky waved the printout with an expansive smile. "It's your line of work. It says here old man Kerrick booked himself a cruise on one of those passenger ships, and you're going along for the ride. You're the best man for the job."

Cocking an eyebrow, Lucky reassured the younger man. "Well, you're not the best, but you're all we got. We'll hunt the old guy down between now and then, try to find him, but if Kerrick gives us the slip, well, we know where he'll be at three o'clock the day after tomorrow. And you'll be right there with him as the ship sails past Lady Liberty. Brody here will get you ready."

Dimmie mopped his face with the back of his hand. "But…But, I…"

Brody kicked Dimmie with his shiny laced shoe, under the desk where Lucky couldn't see, but Dimmie sure felt it and shut his mouth.

Chapter Two

one day previous

Dwarfed by the Manhattan skyscrapers towering above him, the old man glanced at a hot dog vendor on the corner of 7th and 38th Avenue. This late in the day, forget about it. Everybody knew you had to eat a hot dog at the beginning of the lunch rush. Any time after that, you got the foot longs that had been floating in that oily swamp water for who knows how long, maybe not even heated through all the way. The vendor had a line. Tourists, what did you expect? Maybe he'd have time to grab a dog in the morning, before embarkation. Many a time he'd picked a foot long up from the blonde kid on the corner of Broadway and 43rd, but that was too close to Times Square, Irish turf. Would the kid remember him after all these years? He'd better not chance it. Those lumpy braids he had…what were they called?

Dreadlocks, Ellie's voice gently reminded him.

So close to Junior's! His mouth watered just thinking about a piled-high Reuben with that creamy cole slaw...heaven! The diner in Nebraska put vinegar in their cole slaw. Anybody with a mouth knew it had to be buttermilk. And Junior's cheesecake was the best; not buried under soggy strawberries like they had something to hide, but honest cheesecake, tall, with tangy sour cream topping.

He stepped off into an intersection, jumping back as a car raced around the corner. The driver waved his fist, cursing, and the old man smiled. He inhaled the smell of exhaust, bread baking, sausages, and garbage, mixed with expensive aftershaves of a group of businessmen rushing past. The aroma of New York City. Ah, home again!

The old man blotted the corners of his lips, straightened his tie, and turned toward Little Italy. A slice and a glass of vino wasn't the same as Junior's, but he couldn't risk being seen in the old neighborhood. He knew the Irish would not venture into Little Italy, even these days. Things hadn't changed *that* much.

As he walked along the bustling street, he kept an eye on his reflection in the store windows. Anybody following him? You could never be too careful; how often had he said that? No indication anyone was paying any attention to him — he felt nearly invisible in his fedora and nondescript trench coat.

The coat was nearly thirty-seven years old, a gift from Ellie on his fortieth birthday. He'd had that tailor on 43rd street replace the lining a time or two. Funny people, tailors; usually overlooked, like barbers or doormen. People felt free to spill their guts as if they weren't even in the room. A good source of information, he'd learned early on, back when he ran the city. The guy on 43rd was among the best at listening and reporting what he'd heard. That had saved his hide more than once, and kept him abreast of the city's undercurrent as well. A mob boss had to know things.

As he walked, his brows knit at the gang tagging on the walls in some of the alleys. What is the world coming to? *Graffiti,* he corrected himself, but most of it wasn't art at all. Disrespectful young punks called themselves gangs these days. They were nothing but a bunch of hoodlums. No sense of loyalty, no dedication to the family or the way things had always been. Not even a sense of style. Wearing those black hoodies, like they were afraid to show their faces. And spray paint. How much honor was there in a can of spray paint?

When he ran the city, things were different. In the old days, men dressed like men; shirt tucked in, dark necktie, fedoras on the street. Nowadays, every other male in public had his trousers sagging, the waistband a foot too low. What if they needed to run for it? How far would they make it with their pants down around their ankles?

What a turn his life had taken. Here he was, an exile, a tourist in his own city. Not his anymore. He paused to catch his breath, jostled on every side by people on the sidewalk, all intent on their own lives, oblivious to anyone around them. They certainly didn't care about an old man running from his new life, unwelcome in his former life.

Enjoy the life you've been given, Ellie always said. He always amended with a smile, *or the one I take.* Her crooked smile belied the frown in her Irish blue eyes. Eyes so blue he could swim in them. He swiped at his lashes. Must be the wind.

With the ship sailing late tomorrow afternoon, he was determined to cram in as much as he possibly could. At his age, every day was a gift. That's what Ellie always said. How he wished she could be with him, linking her arm through his!

On a whim, he raised his hand and a cab pulled up within seconds.

"Empire State Building." He climbed in the back, careful not to touch any surfaces. Besides being mindful of where he left his fingerprints, the cab was none too clean. They never were. Even so, hailing a cab was satisfying. In Omaha, he stuck out his arm to hail a cab and three people across the street waved back. What a place.

He settled back, his fedora on his lap. A ten-minute ride, this time of day. He didn't bother watching the route; as soon as he spoke, the driver's shoulders sagged. The old man knew it wasn't worth the driver's time to try to add in a few extra blocks and run up the meter, not after hearing his strong New York accent. Probably had the city streets memorized. He'd do better with tourists later on.

The cab stopped with a lurch near the corner of 35th and 5th Avenue. The old man slipped a few bills from his hand-tooled leather wallet, unfolded his legs stiffly, and stood on the sidewalk. Just north of Korea town; he could tell that with his eyes closed, the smell was that strong. Fish and spices Ellie never used. He didn't understand how Asians stayed alive when all they ate was chopped up stringy stuff and a lot of rice. A man liked to see what he was eating. With Asian food, he couldn't even tell what most of the ingredients were. And those people didn't even use forks. How much could you pick up with two little sticks? No wonder they were so skinny.

Skimming the pulsing crowd on the sidewalk, always wary, he turned toward the heavy doors, feeling a whoosh of silence wash over him as the revolving door spit him into the marble lobby. On a rainy or foggy day, there'd be no point in going up to the observation decks, but the heavens were smiling on him today. A clear day, and not much of a wait, either. He paid for an elevator ticket. At $26 a pop, it was highway robbery. Fleecing tourists was a gold mine no matter where you went. Still, the Empire State Building was an icon. He might never get there again, and what did Ellie always say? *Take your chances while you got 'em, they may never come again.*

She also often said *Be where you are.* That made no sense to him for the first few years they were together. Where else could he be, but where he was? One day it dawned on him. Be in the moment, enjoy what you're doing; that's what she meant. Today, he was going to be where he was and that meant overlooking his beloved city. Who knows, it could be his last time.

At his age, anything he did might be his last.

Ticket in hand, he followed the line on the floor to the elevator and, when it opened, took his place with the tourists, holding onto the railing inside. A teenaged girl giggled nervously as the elevator doors closed. Somebody said, "It says here in this brochure it'll take just under one minute to reach the 86th floor."

He wished they'd see if they could hold their breath that long, just so they'd stop their constant chatter. What did they have to talk about anyway? They were probably from Iowa, and everybody knows there's nothing worthwhile in Iowa. A lot like Nebraska, most likely. It was fine with him that they visited his city, but be a little respectful. He glowered at the girl. At least stop giggling, aye.

At last, the elevator doors slid open and he made his way to the observation deck. Oh, how he loved the city! Streets and avenues laid out in a tidy grid pattern, Central Park gleaming like a green gemstone in the center, skyscrapers towering like an intricate puzzle. On a clear day, he'd heard, you could see five states, all the way to Pennsylvania and Connecticut, but he wasn't interested in seeing that far. He'd seen far enough in his lifetime.

The city was what he loved, and from this dizzying height, it looked pristine and orderly. He well knew the underbelly of the city was a dirtier situation. He turned to tell Ellie to *look at the cathedral over there, how small the tower looks from up here, look, you can even see the fountain.* He caught himself.

Ellie is gone.

Chapter three

Ellie is gone.

His heart sighed, skipping a beat. She passed away a couple of months ago, fifty-six days ago, in fact. He could still feel her in his arms that afternoon, her thin frame bird-like. He growled at the sun for shining, but left the ruffled curtains open. She loved the sunlight. He'd have done anything to change places with her, to take away the pain she endured with barely a murmur.

For a while, he wasn't sure she was still with him, her breathing was that shallow. He held his hand under her nostrils, feeling a faint wisp of air. "Don't go, my lass. Bide a while longer..."

Her chest expanded in a deep breath, shuddering. Her eyes opened for the first time in two days. She smiled over his shoulder, past his face, her hand outstretched. "Oh, it's *you!* I knew you'd be here." She squeezed his hand and sighed, "See you around, Darling," and that was that.

He'd wondered many times what did she mean by, "It's *you!*" You, who? It had better not be that numbskull, Donovan McCready. He'd had his eye on her for years. If he found out it was Donovan, he'd bust his chops when he got there, Heaven or not.

He wished he learned to cook. Oh, he could fry an egg well enough, but a man liked a real meal. He'd never been one for packaged food. Some of that canned stuff the home nurse brought in for Ellie could have doubled as dog food, if you didn't like your dog all that much. In the city, it was easy enough to stop at a diner in the morning, a bodega during the day, and, of course, Ellie was a fine cook. Her lamb stew and colcannon could bring a grown man to tears, it was that good.

He took her out to eat as often as he could. He liked showing her off, seeing the admiring glances when she walked in. Sometimes he'd sit back while she talked to the chef, asking how a certain dish was prepared, comparing recipes. A few times, the chef pulled out a chair and the two of them had an animated conversation, like he wasn't even there. The city had the best food in the world, everybody knew that. Why else would so many tourists flock to New York?

Since she died, he'd been going to the diner in town more often, and frying eggs in between. A man can only eat so many eggs before he begins to feel like a chicken, although he knew chickens don't eat eggs. Even so.

He learned how to run the washing machine, but his shirts were never as crisp as he liked them. He'd taken to sending their clothes out when Ellie was too sick to iron them anymore. The white-curled clerk at the dry cleaners was too chatty for his liking. It was easy enough to pretend he didn't understand her. He knew he looked different than the locals; let her think he spoke a foreign language as well.

There was no way he'd stay in the Program, not without Ellie, nor in Nebraska, either. He had hated the assigned house with its perky flowered curtains on sight. It had no character, not like the high rises or brownstones in the city. Boxy, like a child might draw. Of course, the whole place was nothing to write home about, if he'd ever thought about writing home. He didn't even know where home was anymore.

And the sky...the sky was too big for him. It loomed over him in the daytime like a big blue bowl with that relentless hot sun baking all in its reach. Opening the door of the house midday was like aiming one of those beauty salon hair dryers at his face. People said, "It's not so bad. It's a *dry* heat."

Aye, so was Ellie's oven.

And the *wind!* Oh, that wind. During the summer, it sand-blasted his face and blew grit down his collar. Come winter, it blew snow into what the weatherman on channel six called a whiteout. Good word for it, whiteout, furious snow falling hard and nothing to block it. He'd never seen snow like that. In New York, it snowed, then stopped, like it was supposed to. Nebraska's snow was a monster, a malevolent entity determined to bury every bush and car and snowing a few feet deeper for good measure. The winds blew it into drifts higher than the house, blocking the doors and windows, barricading them in from the rest of the world. It was enough to drive a man around the bend.

Ellie had that special laugh that reminded him of bubbles. That first winter, she said something about *Little House on the Prairie*, some book she'd read as a girl. She seemed to think being trapped by their own four walls and a mountain of snow on all sides was a lark. She finally suggested he teach her to play seven-card stud. Poker wasn't ladylike, but she said she had to take his mind off the snow, or he'd wear a hole in the old braided rug. All that pacing.

He wasn't much for reading, never had been, beyond the *New York Times,* of course. He had to keep his finger on the pulse of the city. Even that; he found a newsstand in their new town that carried the paper, but it was always a day late and even later after a storm. The news was stale by the time he read it, but it was better than nothing. Barely.

Almost every morning, before she grew too weak, he and Ellie drove the four miles into what people called a town, barely a wide spot on the two-lane road, to pick up the paper. They often stopped at the diner for some breakfast or pie. One thing the people in Nebraska were good at was making fruit pie. He hadn't been able to find any cheese steak or foot longs or even decent pizza, but the pie was good.

One time, Ellie pointed out cows walking along the side of the fence, walking, walking, walking, single file, nose to tail, all the way down the fence line, like they had somewhere to be. She wondered where they were going. Where do cows have to go? They drove another mile or two and the stupid things were turning back, making a U-turn. Cows were walking east and next to them cows walked west, nose to tail, none of them going anywhere at all.

They chuckled, but he felt a hollow under his ribs. People outside the city were like those cows, thinking they had a life, but going nowhere. Here he was, among them, with no sense of purpose beyond trying to make Ellie smile.

He couldn't even do that at the end.

Nebraska had more birds than he'd ever seen in New York City, different colored ones, too. The only birds he had ever noticed in the city were pigeons. Oh, and those little brown starlings with the annoying cheep cheep cheep. Years ago, when he and Ellie were only a few months into their marriage, she wondered aloud where did baby pigeons come from. She'd never seen a young one, or a nest, either. From then on, he paid attention, and sure enough, they all looked the same to him, no nestlings among the pigeons in the city. When Ellie took sick, she liked to sit in the easy chair facing the window with an afghan around her, watching the birds. He put out birdseed and breadcrumbs to attract them and she would clap her hands in delight. It took so little to make Ellie happy.

Ellie slept a lot those last weeks. It seemed a waste. Once He knew she wouldn't recover, couldn't the Good Lord Above grant her the strength to dance one last time? In her youth, she could cut a rug that'd put those television dance contests to shame. He could still see her flushed face with that million-dollar smile, brushing aside the boys who vied for her attention.

While she slept, he evaluated what he'd need to move forward, to go on living while his heart lay in the cold earth beside his Ellie. The basics: food, clean clothing, a roof over his head. Bonus would include people to talk to, interesting places to see, maybe medical care in case something happened. He thought about adding "a reason for living" to the list. No, when Ellie died, she'd taken that with her.

What could he do, moving forward? How could he go on living when his heart was in the cold ground? What was the point of going on at all? Staying alone in the little yellow house was out, where Ellie drew her last breath. Regret clamped his chest when he thought about it, taking her away from the city she was born in, forcing her to live in a desolate place 3000 miles off the end of any map that matters, away from family and friends she'd had since she was a schoolgirl in pigtails.

That Sinatra fellow knew what he was talking about. Ellie loved New York, the night life, the lights, the constant noise and motion, the heartbeat of a city that never slept. He had taken that away from her. Exiled his beloved in a place as flat as the diner's pancakes and just as monotonous.

Well, it's not as though he had a choice where they put him. His pricy lawyer said anywhere would be an improvement over the penitentiary cell he richly deserved. Lincoln, Nebraska, was barely a city at all, and the Program planted them more than forty miles west to boot. A few miles past nowhere, that's what it was.

No wonder people went mad out here.

Chapter four

Turning state's evidence was the right thing to do, but, oh, how he regretted his actions, replaying in his mind like a B-movie when sleep avoided him. No matter how he looked at it, he'd had no choice. Somebody had to break the cycle of madness. As the kingpin of the organization, the Irish mob boss, it fell to him. In the past, he would never have dreamed of turning in his old friends, his coworkers, his brothers in arms.

It's one thing to take out rivals; that was the business. Everybody understands that. But when Jimmy the Deuce put a hit on that woman on Fifth Avenue, pushing her twin babies in a stroller, and in broad daylight...

Well, that was a line honorable men just don't cross.

And for what? What had she done? Had lunch with the second-in-command's son-in-law; not exactly a capital offense. In the old days, somebody would have been sent to her house to set her straight, and maybe busted the guy's jaw and reminded him of his wife and kiddies at home. But, no, Jimmy had her shot in front of a crowd of stupid tourists with their little flat cameras and it was all over the news that night. The son-in-law's body was never found. It never would be, not where they put him.

No honor at all.

Fuming at home that night, he had spilled his frustrations to Ellie. Ellie was a good woman; bright, but she knew how to keep her mouth shut. She blotted tears as he told her about the young mother killed on the street. Those poor motherless babes. He griped about Vic the Vermin, the Italian mobster who'd turned state's evidence in that corruption and money laundering scheme last year. Several mobsters went to prison over that, serving terms longer than their underlings got for killing innocent people who wouldn't go along, maybe ones who'd seen more than they should have. Where was the honor? What would the old-time bosses think if they could see this, their legacy?

As he paced like a caged lion, Ellie listened as long as she could, then dozed with her head on the grey fringed pillow.

As the sun rose reluctantly over the city, he stood at the window and realized that insurance commercial was right. Life is short. People should have the right to live as they please, support their families, run their businesses instead of caving to the mob's demands. He saw his cronies in a new light, the thugs they were, a far cry from the dignity and code of a generation past. They were dirty, all of them.

He watched Ellie's chest go up and down, her lashes stark against her pale face. With that diagnosis hanging over her, his heart ached. At least she had lived a good long life, not like that young mother.

His mind made up, he took her hand. "Beloved, my lass, wake up. I'm thinking about doing something that wants doing, aye, and I need your blessing."

By testifying, he well knew he was putting himself and his wife at risk, and he put serious thought into it, a week or more of sleepless nights. Ellie held him during the nights when he lay awake, reassuring him he was doing the right thing. What else could he do? There was nothing else he could have done and still called himself a man. She knew what the cost would be. Yet she urged him to speak out, saying what good was honor if no one respected the code anymore? How could he live with himself if he kept silent? He rubbed the back of his hand. He could still feel her soft fingers caressing his arm as he waited for sleep just before dawn.

"You're a good man, Colin Kerrick. You're an honorable man, and if this is the price for maintaining your honor, I am with you. I'll always be with you."

And then she wasn't.

Chapter five

Over and over, the scenario played through his mind, his subconscious searching fruitlessly for a way forward, any other option. The nights were the worst. When he was a boy, he could sleep anywhere, any time, but these last few years, sleep was like a ghost, just out of his reach. Too clearly, he recalled that fine spring day, with Ellie at his side in her best red blouse and skinny blue skirt — she called it a pencil skirt — taking the train to Philly, walking into the FBI office, stopping at the front desk. He held up his briefcase.

"I have something to report."

They made them wait over an hour on those hard wooden chairs. Realizing he wasn't going anywhere, somebody finally sent a junior agent to send him away. With Ellie on his arm there in the lobby, he interrupted, shoved some files under the agent's nose, and repeated, "I have something to report." Say what you will about him; he kept meticulous records and all they needed was right there.

Skimming the first page, the agent blanched. He stammered, "F-f-follow me, this way, please," and barked at the receptionist, "Get me Johnson, Jones, Thomas, Lark, all of them. Grant, too. This is big. Really big."

Talking to him and Ellie took so long, somebody sent out for cheese steaks. They finally put them up in a hotel that night; a decent place, by government standards. It was no five-star, but nice enough, and Ellie was able to sleep at least.

At the trial, the old mob boss ignored the packed house and testified in detail against the eight defendants, calmly detailing enough crimes to keep the fibbies busy for years. Her eyes wide, Ellie sat still as years of ledger pages flashed on the screen. She watched from the front row, her slim shoulders straight, eyes never wavering. When had she become so thin? He hadn't noticed until the second day of testimony, when he looked to her for support. She met his eyes and a smile played on her red lips. She mouthed, "I love you," and new resolve flooded through him.

During it all, Ellie stood with him, nodding encouragement in court, dabbing tears when the photos of the young mother were displayed, larger than life, lying in a pool of blood on the street like a spilled soda. She clung to his arm when they ran the gauntlet of those reporters with their furry microphones after another day of him testifying in court. When the ruling came down, she smiled through her tears, her blue eyes locked on his across the courtroom.

The verdict shook the mob. He knew it would. That night, and for days afterwards, the media talking heads on the television fell all over themselves, trying to get the words out faster than the other outlets. With the mob on shaky ground, the court put him and Ellie in a safe house across the river in Jersey. Within a week, somebody torched their home and it burned to the ground. An accident, the police said.

Ellie silently clutched his hand the day the Feds drove them to the airstrip at Teterboro. She raised a perfect brow when the tall agent told them the car was part of a set of decoy vehicles; not to fear, they'd get them to the airport safely. As if that was the worst of their worries. Tears brimming as they circled the city for the last time, she made a joke about having a posh private plane, not having to deal with those TSA agents at LaGuardia who couldn't keep their hands to themselves.

She dozed at last with her coppery curls on his shoulder. Out of a bottle now, but how he loved her for keeping her red tint all these years. The day she agreed to marry him, he told her he'd never love anybody but a red-headed Irish lass. He'd kept his word; no other woman had ever caught his eye, not like some of other boys. Those men didn't last long in his organization. If a man couldn't keep his vow to his own wife, how could he be trusted in the mob? Once he heard word of infidelity, they were out on their ears. Let them go work in the shops, for all he cared.

He nudged her awake as the earth rose up to welcome them to their new home, the plane losing altitude and coming to a bumpy landing, surrounded by not much at all. He saw his first live cattle as the plane taxied, and hundreds more later that day. The land was flat, and colorless, too, unless you liked green cornstalks for as far as the eye could see. One of the agents in the back of the plane quipped, "Hot enough to pop popcorn in the field."

What had he done? Surely, they weren't expected to make a home here.

Ellie clutched his hand as the hot, dry air hit them when the door swung open. They stepped down the stairs folded out of the plane's clamshell door. She whispered, "Where is everything?" and all he could do was squeeze her hand. The Feds had told them Witness Protection never relocated people to a metropolis, but he figured the rolling plains hadn't changed much since the buffalo roamed this part of the world. He'd seen enough spaghetti westerns to know buffalo liked this terrain.

Himself, he wasn't so sure.

Ellie, on the other hand, was like a spider, like the ones his Nanna talked about in the Old Country. She said a spider would get swept up by the wind or some brat with a stick, and the minute its ugly feet touched something solid, it'd begin to spin a new web, make itself a new home. That's what Ellie did. She made a home, working with what she had. It wasn't nearly as comfortable as their old house in Bay Ridge, but they were together and that's what mattered. Any time he faltered, she reminded him of that.

And falter he did, watching her use her skimpy energy for potting geraniums on the front porch. Occasionally, he noticed her staring across the endless prairie, a wistfulness in her eyes. It felt like a stab wound to his soul. Maybe he'd have felt better if she'd talked about it, but she kept up her cheerful façade. He tried to be upbeat for her sake, his part of the dance during the day, watching her sleeping form by moonlight filtering in through the chintz curtains.

And the culture shock was every bit as rough as his folks endured when they came from old Ireland. He couldn't adapt to his new name, Niall Clancey, on the driver's license they gave him. It sounded like some cartoon character, and he tired of correcting people he met. Niall was a good Irish name, not Egyptian; *Niall*, not Nile.

He never did call Ellie by her new name. To him, she was Ellie, not Josephine, no matter how many times the agents corrected him.

Any time he opened his mouth, people stared like they'd never heard the lilt of a brogue before, or a New York tinge, either. He missed the non-stop energy of the city, and living in a one-traffic-light town was boring. That wasn't true, he allowed; it had three stoplights. He'd counted.

What had he done to her? Ellie went downhill fast, too fast, once the diagnosis was confirmed, although the Feds kept their word and she had the best doctors money could buy. Even a specialist flown in a couple of times. Some doctor; he held his white hanky over his nose and mouth, as if he was unwilling to let the dust of the plains sully his pinched nostrils.

While Ellie lay in the hospital bed with the too-white sheets, Colin put a lot of thought into what he'd need. She was going to die, he couldn't deny it. They'd fought it as long as they could.

He'd heard about some new experimental treatments in the doctor's waiting room from other desperate family members who were on the same death vigil as he. Nobody was going to experiment on his wife, not so long as he was alive and breathing. When they said there was nothing more they could do for her, he took her back to the little yellow house.

To die.

Chapter six

A bed, food, new people to interact with, that's all he needed, and someone to tidy up after him. Maybe some travel. Since he came from the Old Country in 1957, the old man had hardly left American soil. He'd been working those years, keeping his finger in every pie. But now…Who would notice if he up and walked away? His minder checked on him like clockwork, every Wednesday morning, whether he needed it or not. Perfunctory, no heart in it. He'd never have kept a man on in the Organization with a work ethic as low as that. Not for a New York minute.

Ellie always said, when you have only one choice, make it. She also quoted Yogi Berra, who said, "When you come to a fork in the road, take it." Either way, don't look back; no second-guessing. So he took the only choice he saw.

He had to time his run right. Good thing his Program minder was such a loser. The oily little man came like clockwork; he hadn't ever made contact once between scheduled visits, and never stayed more than five minutes when he did show up. He didn't know where the guy came from, but it wasn't worth the trip. He couldn't call him "Agent Smith," although that's what his business card insisted his name was. *Smith*, indeed. A minder he was, no agent at all, and not the brightest light on Broadway. The greasy man left his smudged business card on the kitchen counter every single time, as if he and Ellie couldn't be trusted to remember who he was.

The old man had heard of other guys in the Program, ones who made their way to freedom, who had good agents who actually listened to them, helped them, acted like they cared. Old McGuinn's agent even helped him make a run for it, and only asked for eighteen per cent of the money McGuinn had hidden at his aunt's place in Jersey. Now, that was a man with honor. At least, he was until he turned McGuinn in at the state line.

What can you do? Everybody has to make a living.

He knew he couldn't count on Smith or whatever his name was to come through in a pinch. The guy had so little respect, he barely even made eye contact. Even when they told him Ellie's diagnosis, he only nodded and made a note in his little black spiral notebook. He'd never help out an old man; he's just waiting for him to die off so he can get him off his roster. What kind of man gets himself exiled to *Nebraska* of all places? Anyone knew the Feds' action was in DC or New York.

He'd heard about those old folks' homes, where people went to die when they had no family to take them in. He had no one, but he wasn't as bad off as all that. So long as he could drive to the newsstand and tie his own tie with a proper Windsor every morning, he didn't need any 24-hour care. He had enough money in the bank to live comfortably, plus a good amount elsewhere the Feds hadn't found out about. He just needed somebody to take over the household tasks that Ellie had always handled.

Every day when Colin headed to the diner, he passed that billboard showing a glowing image of the Keep The Heart Close assisted living home *For Those In The Golden Years*. There wasn't much gold left in his years, he knew, but he was curious. And bored; what else did he have to fill his days?

One morning after pie and coffee at the diner, he walked to the sprawling complex on Fourth Street. As he surveyed Keep The Heart Close from a bench by the sidewalk, an efficient-looking woman bustled out of the front door and took him by the arm.

"Come along, sweetie, it's nearly lunch time, and I know how much you older gentlemen love your tapioca pudding." Ignoring his protests, she hauled him by the arm into the hotel-like building, down a musty hall and deposited him at a table with three older men. She was stronger than she looked.

Hunched over the oilcloth covered table, one of the old men traced a line of grease with gnarled fingertip. "First timer, huh? They'll have you in line in no time. They get us all in the end," with a rusty laugh.

The others stared into space. One idly plucked a petal from the dusty plastic flower arrangement in the middle of the table. He licked the petal, then sat back as a white-aproned woman set soup bowls in front of each of them.

The greasy sheen turned Colin's stomach, but he gamely dipped his spoon, recoiling at the taste. Dishwater, and barely warm. Ellie never scolded him for preferring his soup steaming hot. He'd heard some other wives refused to serve it hot enough, no matter what their husbands liked. Not Ellie.

He blotted his lips with the rough paper napkin and pushed back his chair.

The apron lady bumped him back into it before he could get his feet under him to stand. "Now, now, you can't leave us," she cooed in a voice as sticky as syrup. "You don't want to miss your nice noodles." She set a plate of stringy spaghetti under a smear of grayish-red sauce in front of each of the men at the table. They dug in, slurping the mushy pasta as if they hadn't eaten in a week. He poked his fork into the gummy noodles, waiting until the woman walked through a doorway, then bolted for the front door.

He maintained a goodly clip until he reached the safety of the town square. Mopping his brow as he caught his breath on a cedar bench, he shook his head. He hoped he wouldn't live long enough to think Keep The Heart Close was a viable option. It'd drive him to murder, and he already had plenty of those on his soul.

Chapter seven

The morning after seeing Keep The Heart Close, the old boss sat in the diner, his coffee untouched, the paper spread out on the worn Formica tabletop. Turning to the City Living section of the paper, a full-page ad caught his eye. A travel agency promoted a New England cruise, touting the amenities on the cruise ship in living color.

His heart raced. What about moving onto a cruise ship? He could book one after the other, or maybe change ships at the end of a cruise or two. That's the ticket. Like a retirement home, without a home at all.

A cruise ship had everything he needed. A clean room with turn down service, 24-hour-a-day food—and the good stuff, not grey slime—a nightly show, new places to see, a new batch of people boarding every week, new faces to talk to, if he felt like talking to anybody. There'd be a casino, and even a shuffleboard court onboard. He had a talent for poker, no denying that. And he'd enjoyed playing shuffleboard with the old guys in Florida on their last vacation, but not enough to move down there. Funny thing about Florida; the farther south they drove, the more New York accents they heard. Maybe they should have moved there; maybe Ellie would have still been alive in the tropical sunshine. Nebraska was no place for a girl from the city.

Too late for that now. He shook off the thought, brushed it from his mind like lint from a jacket.

Ellie loved the city as much as he did, but she had an itchy foot. Every summer, she insisted on a vacation, usually to Rockaway Beach or the Jersey shore. A couple of years, when business made it impossible for him to get away in August, he'd taken her to New England as a special treat once things slowed down. She complained mildly, wondering aloud how it was that the mob had a busy season.

Once there, she marveled at the colors. Mainers called their trees with autumn leaves *the colors*, as if they'd cornered the market on God's biggest crayon box. That's what Ellie said. Their driver took them to a lobster shack on a tiny bay. Ellie loved it. She clapped her hands when they served dinner; a giant red lobster apiece, a dish of melted butter, a basket of warm rolls, and a pile of paper napkins. A man with a yellow plastic apron showed them how to eat the lobster. Colin smiled, remembering Ellie's bright face with melted butter smearing her red lipstick, her eyes dancing at the novelty of eating outdoors, and with her hands, too. Oh, how he missed her!

Living on a cruise ship sounded ideal, the more he thought about it. All he really needed was someone to prepare his food and keep the place clean behind him. Make his bed. He didn't need a large home; a ship's stateroom would suit him well enough. One with a picture window, maybe a balcony. No, a suite. He could afford that. Growing up in a city made of concrete, he'd never developed an interest in gardening or mowing the lawn, so he'd be fine in a small place. The more he thought about it, the better it sounded. Seeing unending ocean would beat the flat, never-ending prairie. A cruise ship never had that piercing squall of tornado warning sirens every afternoon, either. He wouldn't know a soul, and no one would know him. He could make up a whole new persona, now that he knew what that was like. Lose the Niall moniker once and for all.

He cradled his cup to the little living room, not even seeing the flowered chintz curtains that came with the house. He sat in the stiff recliner as long as his back could stand it, weighing his options. A cruise ship had everything he'd need, even laundry service and a doctor onboard. It'd cost about a quarter of what Keep The Heart Close charged. There'd be free entertainment and a staff to meet his needs.

First, he'd better check it out. Maybe a trans-Atlantic cruise? The thought of all that empty ocean all at once made his stomach lurch under his starched shirt. He'd better try a shorter cruise first. The ad's New England itinerary began in New York and headed into Boston and north to Bar Harbor, Portland, Saint Johns, and Halifax before looping back south. With his mined open, he'd see if he could live on a ship permanently, like a retirement package with no physical address, one back-to-back cruise after another. Closing his eyes, he shuddered. Those poor old men in the old folks' home. Not him, he'd be living the high life on a cruise ship before long. He knew, once he left the Program, there'd be no turning back.

The Feds had made that clear.

Chapter eight

On Tuesday afternoon, he had lunch in the diner, same as always—Tuesday was Hot Turkey Sandwich day—then walked two blocks to the public library. Sitting on a bench in the deserted courtyard, he made a phone call to the travel agent in the newspaper. The woman told him going on a cruise by himself would cost nearly double, something about a solo surcharge. She suggested he "pick up a honey to share" his cabin. Drawing a breath, he nearly hung up on the syrupy voice, but he had his mind made up. He drummed his fingers as she cooed something about a man of his advanced years being in demand on a cruise ship. Why, some lines even paid elderly men to be dance partners, make sure the widows have a good time on board. Did he want her to make a note of that for the cruise line?

He held back a sharp retort; he knew gigolos in the city, and that wasn't for him. Besides, he hadn't cut a rug in a long time, not since Ellie took sick. In the end, he booked a suite, cabin 906 on the *Ocean Serenity* in his own name, and even swung a steep discount because it was a last-minute booking.

In cruise lingo, "last-minute" meant within ninety days of the sailing date, and this one left two weeks from Saturday, out of New York's Manhattan Terminal. He'd have left that very night, if he could have. Once his mind was made up, he liked to move and move fast. With Ellie gone, the walls closed in on him. He didn't know how a shoebox-sized place could echo that badly, but when she died, she took the life right out of the house with her.

Tired of hiding like some criminal, he determined to use the name his mother had given him. He'd need a new passport, and a good one, too. He didn't dare call on his old contacts to make new ID, especially not in his real name, a name he suspected would still cause waves if anyone in the mob heard it.

He'd started playing poker with some old guys on Thursdays. He had nothing in common with them and no need of friends; just a way to pass an evening. After a few beers, Sam mentioned his great-grandson had showed him his fake ID card he bought to buy booze on weekends.

"Josh's mother would kill him if she knew, but that's one advantage to being old. There's two generations between me and anybody who should do something about it." Smothering a cough, Sam laughed. Cigarettes would be the death of him.

A few hands later, the old man managed to turn the conversation back to Sam's grandson. Who'd he find to make him the fake ID? You wouldn't think there'd be a need for that kind of business in a town this small.

"You know that new tattoo parlor over on the east side? Some guy name of Ray made it for him. Wait'll his mother sees the tattoo Josh got on his back while he was there. That boy better keep his shirt on, that's all I got to say. Young people these days. You gonna play or hold 'em or what?"

Colin took the hand, and took note of the tattoo parlor, too. He made a stop there the next morning, right after he picked up the paper. Ray took a step back; he wasn't used to payments of that size. His words spilled over each other as he said he'd work fast to get the passport done and done right.

Money talked, even in Nebraska.

Chapter nine

On schedule, Colin's minder came, checked a few boxes on his clipboard without even making eye contact and drove away in his fancy sedan, likely paid for with hard-working Americans' tax money. He never even mentioned Ellie. It wasn't likely that "Agent Smith" would notice Colin was gone for a week at least, unless he made a random phone call. Agents were supposed to do that several times a week, but the calls stopped a couple of weeks after they came to Nebraska.

Even so, Colin had booked his flight out of Des Moines, not Omaha, direct to LaGuardia airport. Shaking his head at the size of the Midwest states again, he squared his shoulders and settled in for the three-hour drive. It wasn't like New England, where a person could drive through four or five states and be back by lunchtime. He'd had no need to drive in New York, but he'd practiced in Nebraska in the sedan the Feds provided with the house.

Their first month there, he and Ellie took classes from the Drivers' Education place in town, mostly out of boredom. Ellie said they had to try new things, be where they were. He could still hear her giggling as she nearly hit that tree, one of the few in town. "It tried to jumped in front of me, did you see that?" A suicidal tree; that'd be the day.

Still, practicing driving gave them something to do on the endless afternoons, a change of scenery, she said, not that there was any scenery to speak of. She was pretty good at it, until one day she said she was too tired. The car had sat in the garage since then.

He didn't seriously think anybody bothered putting a tracking device in the tan sedan —where would anybody expect an old couple like him and Ellie to go? — but he took the precaution of telling his poker-playing cronies his car was going in the shop next Thursday. As he expected, Sam instantly offered him the loan of his car. "Come get it whenever you want it," without even asking where he was going. Some people. He'd park Sam's car in the long-term parking lot at the airport. Somebody would find it eventually, but with a bit of luck, he'd have a few days' head start.

He watched the taillights of Agent Smith's car turn at the corner. Good riddance. He polished off the canned soup left over from last night's dinner, wiped up the toast crumbs and washed out his bowl, propping it on the sideboard to dry. Straightening his tie, he walked down the block and borrowed Sam's station wagon. The keys were under the mat, as promised. Returning to the yellow house, he pulled the car into the garage and pushed the button, closing the overhead door.

In his bedroom, he dragged the wheeled suitcase into the living room. He double-checked his carry-on bag. Examining his brand-new passport again, he bent the cover a bit so it didn't seem so fresh. Given a bonus big enough to keep his mouth shut, Ray had made the new passport in only two days. He did good work, too. Quality was quality, and this guy was a real artist. He wished he could show it to Ellie. She appreciated art. He patted his prescriptions.

Gullible druggist had given him 90-days' worth of each without question. People were so trusting. By the time three months were up, he'd be in a new place and settled, like one of those spiders, spinning a new home for himself.

Moving through each room one last time, pulling the blinds against the sunshine, he paused in the bedroom. Could he smell Ellie's perfume? No. Maybe he should have kept a few of her dresses or something that belonged to her, but those ladies from the church with the tarnished steeple had bustled in and taken over after Ellie's funeral and he'd let them.

Buried under the cold ground, with a grave marker in a false name. At the time, he'd debated putting her real name, Ellie Mavis Kerrick, on the gravestone, but the people around town would have badgered him, demanding explanations, and he wasn't up to that. She was as gone as if she'd never lived on earth.

He hauled his suitcase to the garage and hefted it into the back of the station wagon. He drew a breath and clicked the little button to open the garage door. Easing the car out, he glanced in every direction, making sure no one was watching. Old habits die hard. He paused at the bottom of the driveway and took one last look at the yellow house. Already, it seemed to sag, its usefulness ended.

Booking a cruise out of New York City was a risk, but what were the chances anybody'd see him? He'd avoid his own stomping grounds, at least the places he knew the mob frequented. Eight point five million people called New

York home, and that didn't include tourists on the street. No way would anybody spot one old man.

Ellie was been on his mind lot lately, constantly, even more than right after she passed away. Sometimes he heard her voice in the house and he talked back to her, asking her opinion and so forth as if she was still there. She hadn't said so, but he was sure she'd approve of a cruise. She knew he hated the Program.

He and Ellie had only been on two cruises before, one to Bermuda, another to the Canadian Maritimes and Montreal. By following in their footsteps, or in their wake, so to speak, it'd be a good way for him to feel Ellie near, maybe heal his soul. She always wanted to go on another cruise. Where had the years gone? Why hadn't he made more time for her? On their first cruise, to Bermuda from Bayonne pier in New York City, they woke to snow on the balcony. He didn't understand why it wasn't hot (everyone knew that cruises were tropical and warm), but they laughed and sipped hot cocoa, shivering in bed. Every day was like a honeymoon with her.

He swallowed a tear and turned east. At least, he thought it was east and that's what the compass on the dashboard said. With nothing to look at for miles except cornfields and cows, there were no landmarks.

Ellie was the best wife anybody had ever had, his dearest friend. Besides being beautiful, she knew how to keep her mouth shut and to stay out of the family business. He wished they had had children. Ellie would've been a great mother. It was the one thing he hadn't been able to give her. He'd never thought about being alone in his old age. From the time they met at the USO, he and Ellie planned on growing old together, and they'd done a pretty good job of it. Until the Big C hit, that is.

Passing a dusty pickup truck, he snorted. His minder said the folks in the main office think he dwells too much on the past. Maybe he needs a therapist to get over his wife, Smith said, and they're willing to pay for it, like it was some great gift. Heck, they're willing to pay for everything. They own him.

Lawd-a-mercy, Ah'm free at last

Chains fallin' off 'a my soul

Mercy, mercy, Ah'm free at last

The old Southern spiritual played in his mind, the refrain like a breeze through his soul.

He'd heard it every Sunday from the church across the street from the diner. He and Ellie learned to finish their meal quickly when they belted out that song. It meant less than ten minutes from now, an invasion of well-dressed old women on the arms of well-dressed old men, bent on a feast after services, would pour into the diner. The ROMEO club, they called themselves; Retired Old Men Eating Out. They convened at the diner every Thursday for turkey and poker, and on Sundays, their wives joined them for fried chicken, cole slaw, and pie.

Lawd-a-mercy, Ah'm free at last.

Chapter ten

New York City

Colin picked up a cup of coffee and a black and white from a tiny shop by the hotel. The clerk barked at him and he swallowed a grin. Ah, New York. Sensing Ellie's raised eyebrow—she always insisted he have a good breakfast—he silently promised he'd have a better lunch. Or dinner, at least. His arm ached; maybe he'd slept on it wrong, that's what Ellie would have diagnosed.

Or it could still be cramped from yesterday's flight. Flying sure wasn't what it used to be, aye. In the old days, people dressed up like it was an occasion. Yesterday, he'd seen several passengers wearing what looked like flannel pajamas. And years ago, the stewardesses fell over themselves making sure passengers were happy. They'd keep his glass full and bring by a hot meal. Two, if the flight was longer, and dessert later on. These days, they insisted on being called flight attendants and barely cracked a smile. The seats were too small, and as for getting a nice pillow and blanket, forget about it.

He threw the paper cup in the trash and headed toward the One train station. Battery Park was at the end of the line. He knew the city's street layout like the back of his hand. How else could he send his men where they needed to be? They counted on him to know everything, almost like a father. Not a godfather. The Italians used that word, not the Irish.

This was only the second or third time in his life he'd taken a subway; he'd relied on a driver in the old days. This time of day, the subway was likely faster than sitting in a cab in traffic. When he fumbled at the electronic ticket kiosk, a young man in a bandana stepped up and offered to help navigate the machine. He handed the old man a ticket and his change, minus two dollars, which the younger man deposited in his pocket with a flourish.

A man's gotta make a living.

As the grimy subway ground to an abrupt stop, a mechanized voice intoned, "End of the line. All passengers must exit." Following the other stragglers, he walked down the platform and up the concrete stairs, blinking when the sunlight hit his eyes. He stopped, leaning against a railing catching his breath.

Over a decade later, he could still see this place on 911, the day his city took one to the heart. Terrorists attacked innocents right on American soil with no honor at all. He straightened his tie. Those people shouldn't have even been in America; they had no right. At least in the old days, when the Irish and Italian and even German immigrants came over, they had sponsors, a job waiting for them, the promise they'd make good in their new homeland. Now people slipped in under the fence and expected Lady Liberty to take care of them, while trying to change what she stood for, bending it to their own image. If they wanted America to be like where they came from, why did they ever leave home?

A man who couldn't meet his enemy face to face was no man at all in his book. So little honor left in the world. Killing innocent people; for what? He remembered the sirens wailing for hours that sunny September day, into the night, followed by a tangible silence that felt like it would never end. Worst was the piercing mechanical chirping from hundreds of warning sensors on first responders bemoaning a fallen warrior, keening until the batteries faded, one by one.

And the thick dust after the Twin Towers came down, all the awful grey dust that blew into every crease and crevice. What if it was the ashes of some poor soul? Cremated, dead and cremated, for the crime of showing up to work on time.

Sacred dust.

Once he was allowed back in the building, he'd gingerly blown the particles off the big blue ledger on his desk so he could open it, but the rest he left untouched. He barked at the cleaning lady who came to work nearly a week late. That haunted look in her eyes seared his soul; he'd seen it in the eyes of his fellow New Yorkers. He knew she was only there because she needed the money. He'd given her a couple thou from his wallet and sent her away, leaving him alone in the company of souls he'd never meet. Months later, Ellie finally convinced his to let her dust his office, give those souls a proper resting place. Not on top of his metal filing cabinet.

The big triage center set up on the tip of the island was seared in his memory. He remembered watching the first responder teams racing to Battery Park, setting up triage tents and supplies to treat the walking wounded from the Towers, ferries and small boats converging to evacuate the survivors, people who never came. Sorrowful thing, two days later when they folded up their tents. News media set up camp there, too, waiting for first-hand interviews, wiping tears of their own, frantically trying to track down their own family members in between live shots. Oh, the anguish of the city when its heart literally skipped a beat! But it kept on going; dusted itself off and rose to the occasion.

New York was a survivor. So was he; there was no choice.

He moved into the Staten Island ferry building and listened. He knew there would be a tourist within earshot, asking where to pay for the ferry. There was always one in every crowd. He smiled as he heard a woman.

"Harry, we didn't buy our tickets. Harry..."

Ellie used to take his arm and smile, the game complete. The ferry was another perk of living in the city. Anybody could ride, just by walking on; millionaire or pauper.

Ellie called it "a poor man's cruise and harbor tour." They took the ferry a couple of times a month when they lived in the city. The best time of day was in the early evening when the sun's colors bloomed on the faces of the windowed sky scrapers. They'd admire the glint of light on the skyscrapers, then turn around to face the Statue of

Liberty standing in the harbor with her torch still raised in welcome, even after all she'd seen. The water dancing in the sun's fading rays, tourists and locals alike staring at Lady Liberty, his beloved on his arm, made his heart swell, every time.

A child's laughter pulled him back to the present. A little girl in a pink dress ran past, keeping a step ahead of her mother's outstretched arm. He adjusted his fedora and made his way to the ferry terminal. People pressed him on every side in the large building. Some, he knew, were New Yorkers on their daily commute or shopping trips. Others, the slow-moving ones, were probably tourists. Four thousand rode the ferry at a time; there was room for him, too.

That shrill woman kept saying over and over, "Harry, we didn't buy our tickets, Harry, we didn't buy..." Shaking his head, he felt a pang for poor Harry. To have to listen to that whining voice at home would be unbearable. Maybe Harry was deaf.

On the other hand, at least Harry wasn't alone in the world.

Heart heavy, he took a seat inside the ferry, his view muted by grimy windows. The ride took forever; without Ellie, the ferry was just a boatful of strangers. What a turn his life had taken. Here he was, alone, an exile, a visitor in his own city. At the end of the line, he circled directly back into the terminal and boarded the same boat back to Manhattan. Again, he sat inside the cabin, eyes on the pock-marked floor. What was the point? Coming here was a mistake.

He took the One train back to 42nd street, nodding his thanks to a young man with a blue Mohawk, a black leather briefcase, and wires going to or from his ears like a robot. The world these days, but the man had helped him buy a ticket and he appreciated it. At his age, technology fought back. Gone were the subway ticket-sellers of years past, tucked like bees in honeycomb cells, rows of them, taking dimes without a glance.

Colin breathed a lungful of exhaust as he came out onto the street level. He caught a glimpse of himself in a shop window and, without thinking, tipped his fedora to the image. An old man he was now, but not too old to start a new life.

He'd done that twice already.

Chapter eleven

Lucky Callahan banged his coffee mug on the counter, swearing under his breath. He dipped his paper napkin in the glass of ice water and held it against his burned fingers. Maggie came on the run. "Mr. Callahan, what's the matter? What can I do?" She mopped the spreading liquid with a stained towel.

"What does a guy have to do around here to get a decent cup of coffee? What is this sludge, anyway? It looks like somebody spit in it."

"I made it special for you." Maggie stammered, "It's a mocha hazelnut macchiato with steamed almond milk foam. Caramel drizzle. I read about it in a magazine. I thought you'd enjoy something new."

"New? I ain't got time for something new. Get me a cup of joe and I mean now." Lucky growled. *New.* That was the last thing he needed. In fact, it was trying to move the mob forward with new ideas that got him in this mess to begin with. What was wrong with the old ways?

Maggie dropped the sodden wad of paper and scurried across the diner like a scared rat, returning in under a minute with steaming mug and a slice of pie. She offered a tentative smile, but Lucky didn't glance up. Mr Callahan was a good tipper, but she sighed, knowing she'd lost that revenue stream, at least until he forgot about the coffee.

Lucky stared at the moving mass of people on 42nd street, taking the pulse of the city through the fly-specked window. In the fading light, the stream of tourists and workers heading home blurred together, surging through the city's arteries like blood through a monster. Before long, the street lights would flicker on and the night would come alive. The people of the night would emerge, while others hurried to finish whatever it was they did and get indoors to wait out the dark night. Dark? New York was never really dark. What did they say about the city that never slept? They had no idea what went in the night, most of the camera-toting neck-craners who booked expensive Manhattan hotels to lay down their heads.

Tourists tended to head for the shadows after Broadway shows, while his men would just be starting their workday. He didn't have a lot of tolerance for tourists; they got in his way and clogged the streets, rubber-necking on the sidewalks, adding to the traffic they'd talk about when they went home.

The swarms of clueless people trying to find their way to who knows where slowed him down. How could so many people be so lost? Still, they brought in money, and the more they spent, the more he was able to take from businesses who paid for protection. He put up with them during the day, just barely.

As darkness fell, Lucky came into his own. His favorite time was around 2 am, when the tourists had gone to bed in their classy hotel rooms and working folks were in bed. His men did their best work in the night. When the sun came up, they'd scurry like roaches when the lights switched on, trading places with out of town visitors who greeted the dawning day, eager to cram in as much sight-seeing as possible.

Sipping his coffee, Lucky watched the blur of the milling crowd walking, walking. Ever since he was a boy, he loved to sit and watch the flow of people, feeling the heartbeat of the city. *His* city. The mob had taken a hit a few years ago after Colin Kerrick had testified for the Feds.

He shook his head, marveling for the millionth time at the gall of the old man, turning on his compadres after a lifetime in the mob. The old man sold out his own men, calmly testifying in court, saying what was best left unsaid, giving details and photos and all, unmoved by the hatred in the eyes of the goons in the gallery. Kerrick had to know many of his cronies would never see the light of day again once he finished his speech. Men he came up with, condemned by his calm words. How did he live with himself?

While Kerrick's betrayal shook the ranks, it had been a good thing for Lucky. He had been positioning himself for years, so that, when it was over, he was able to rise swiftly to the top. He knew some of his men still thought of him as "the little boss," unwilling to let go of Kerrick's title of Boss. Yet, here he stood at the top of the heap, the most important man in the underworld, and he ruled his domain with a hard fist and pleasure. Well, the Irish area anyway. He had insiders infiltrating the Italian mob as well. *Infiltrating.* Old Mrs Vincente, his high school English teacher, would smile at that big word. She didn't smile no more, not since she heckled him in the restaurant that day, telling him he'd never amount to anything. He'd showed her.

The animosity went way back, and he didn't know why. The Italians and the Irish were both Catholic, but when they came to New York early on, they were on the outs and never quite got over it. The Irish were never on good terms with the Russians who hated the Ukrainians and the South Americans were trying to weasel their way in, and don't even think about the Asians.

And then you get the young punks coming up, the ones with no respect, no sense of the way things were supposed to be. Maybe old man Kerrick was right. Maybe times were changing too fast. No respect.

Lucky stabbed his fork into the apple pie. Nothing more American than apple pie, and the diner made a pretty good one.

What the heck is almond milk, anyway? Almonds don't give milk.

Cows, they give milk.

Chapter twelve

New York City

Lucky wiped his lips with his paper napkin, threw some cash on the table and slipped into his trench coat. He patted the pistol back into place in a holster under his arm. His girl was pretty good with a needle and thread. She'd built the holster right into the coat. He glanced at his reflection in the mirror by the register. You couldn't even tell it was there.

Third Monday of the month, when he'd go over the take from the previous weeks and see where his boys could apply a little more pressure on the local businesses to increase their portion. Last month was down a little, what with that new chain store opening on 33rd. Those big corporations didn't understand the way things were, the way they'd always been in the city. Ah, well, they could always lean a little harder on the small places.

Out on the street, he waited a couple of minutes for a cab to stop, then shrugged. The subway knit under the city, and it'd be faster this time of night anyway. He made his way down the block to the One train, planning on taking it north back to the club. His driver had a wedding to go to, and Lucky had generously given him the night off. Not every day your sister marries the right kind of guy; it was worth celebrating, and worth the hassle of taking the One. He shrugged. *Give me a chance to see the underbelly of my city*, the parts he missed from the back of his armored black sedan.

In the glaring lights underground, a busker caught his attention, one of those street performers. The violinist swept her bow in wide arcs, eyes closed. She was pretty good, he had to admit, and that slinky black dress did a favor to her figure. Lucky reached into his pocket to drop a couple bills into the open violin case on the dirty concrete floor. Glancing up as the One train southbound pulled into the station, his eyes skimmed the crowd. A person had to keep his wits about him; he'd learned that early on.

A man stepping onto the southbound made him do a double-take. From the back, something about the guy looked familiar. Thin shoulders under the grey trench coat, fedora in place, paper bag in hand…One of the old guard, no doubt, a retired cop, maybe. Lucky watched the old man step onto the subway train, jostled by a group of youth. He reached for a handrail, turning slightly. Lucky drew in his breath.

It couldn't be...after what was it, six years?

No way.

That nose. He'd never forget that nose, which he personally saw old Archie McCain break for Colin Kerrick in a bar fight more than fifteen years ago. The old man never could wear sunglasses again with it bent left like that, but poor Archie got the worst of it.

Hitting the up-and-coming boss like that, the boys saw to it he was wearing cement shoes in the East River before morning. Archie hadn't even put up a fight or nothing. He knew he'd crossed a line and that was that.

Lucky lunged toward the southbound, the doors closing while he still had a couple of yards to go. But how could it be Colin Kerrick? The old man had testified, spoken against his own in a court of law, and he'd been stupid to do it. Guess Colin was one of the lucky ones; few who testified against the association lived to see another sunrise. The FBI used an elaborate series of decoy vans to spirit old Colin out of the city to heaven only knew where. Witness protection swallowed him whole, everything but his history, and Lucky did all he could to erase the last bits of that.

How could Kerrick be back in the city? How could he dare step foot on the mob turf after what he did? Lucky reached in his pocket as the northbound pulled in. Never mind catching the train; he some calls to make.

He smashed his fist into the club's cement wall twenty minutes later, shaking off the sharp pain. Except for Ricky, every one of his men had checked in. Not one of them was close enough to jump on the One train. Each of them had hurried to the stop nearest him, but not in time. Colin Kerrick had given them the slip, and Lucky was livid. He swept the lamp off his desk, ignoring the flying glass shards when it struck the floor.

Not long afterwards, Ricky rushed in from the wedding reception. He was the last to report the old guy somehow vanished into the night. Although Lucky told him and told him to come and stand in front of him like a man,

Ricky preferred to stand in the doorway, where he could lean on the door frame and make a quick getaway in case Lucky threw something. Nobody talked about the dents in the wall where people who dared cross Lucky in times past had managed to duck. Lucky's arm was legendary.

Why, in another life, he could have played pro ball.

"Don't worry, Boss," Ricky assured him. "We got our best tech guys, the IT gurus, on it. One good thing about all those RedyGuard Spec traffic cameras the city put up, we got guys who can tap into the feeds and run facial recognition. If it was even him, I mean." How could it be? Ricky figured Lucky was mistaken; nobody was foolish enough to come back to the City after turning state's evidence, not even old Kerrick. Lucky wasn't old, not like old man Kerrick, but maybe his eyesight was going out. The lighting was none too good near the subways.

"Didn't your momma teach you to talk English? I don't even know what you're talking about. All I gotta say is, somebody better find out where he went." Voice rising, Lucky bellowed, "I saw him, I know it was Colin Kerrick, I tell you it was him. I want him snuffed out before I eat my lunch tomorrow. Who does he think he is? It's *my* city now. How dare he step foot in *my* city?"

With Lucky still shouting, Ricky fled. Something crashed against the wall as he turned the corner.

That arm.

Chapter thirteen

After a sleepless night, Lucky called his crew in before dawn. Rubbing their eyes and smothering yawns, they listened and nodded. And then the excuses began.

Two of the boys had to be downtown at the federal courthouse to make sure the case was going to come out their way and to lean on the attorneys if it looked like it might not. Three of them had been tasked with trailing the Italians who'd been encroaching on their turf. Gambling was one thing, but nobody held a game inside the Irish territory. They had to be reminded that could not continue; the sooner, the better. With the other three still in Jersey cleaning up that mess from last week and Little Joe laid up with a gunshot wound to his hip, Lucky found himself shorthanded.

But this couldn't wait. If Colin Kerrick dared step foot in the city, who knows what he might try next? Lucky wasn't risking any uprising. "Squash it and squash it now" — that was his way.

He sat back in his chair and surveyed his crew. With everybody tied up in one thing or another, that left only Ricky and Dimmie. Lucky took a chance going out last night without his right-hand man, and look what happened. He needed Ricky beside him. The city wasn't a safe place if old Kerrick was back. Who knows what the old boss was up to this time? That left Dimmie.

Lucky stared at the papers on his desk, then at his hitman across the room. If Dimmie had been wearing boots, he'd have been quaking in them. Not a large man to begin with, if anything, he seemed to be getting smaller, shrinking in his own shirt. Sweat beaded on his forehead as he studied the ragged carpet. Lucky sighed; the one sure thing about Dimmie was his name. He'd earned it.

At a knock, Ricky jerked open the office door.

The man at the door blurted, "It's him, all right. We got a picture of him crossing the street by Foley Square. And we got his plans, too. He bought some tickets using his *own name.*"

Ricky took the papers, shutting the door in the man's face. Wordlessly, Ricky passed them to Lucky, grainy photographs obviously run through a fax machine.

Lucky crowed, "It's him. I told you. What did I tell you? I told you it was him, I knew it. I'd know that face anywhere, even this bad side shot." He read the lines scrawled under the photograph. "Used his own name, he did. What's that word? Broozen? Brazen? Whatever, he must be pretty sure of himself, and we gotta stop him."

He glanced at each of the men in the room in turn, and a slow smile spread across his face. He pointed at the visibly perspiring Dimmie.

"Dimmie, my boy, it looks like you're going on a luxury cruise."

Chapter fourteen

Lucky tapped his manicured nails on the desk. "Awright, men, if Kerrick gets on the ship, our boy Dimmie here will be on it, too. Make him blend in, Brody, look good, lay low. Get him some clothes and teach him how to behave. Good luck with that."

He cocked an eyebrow. "If Kerrick gets past us, Dimmie, you'll have to snuff him out." He grabbed Dimmie's shoulder. "Stop yer sniveling. It's a *hit*, like any other. You've done it a hundred times or more. All you gotta do is get on the ship, find the old man, and end it once and for all." *And I'll finally be out of the old man's shadow.*

He pointed at Brian. "You, get on that computer of yours. Get Dimmie on that ship, I don't care how. This paper says the ship has a sea day, then goes to Portland, Maine, Bar Harbor, Halifax, Saint Johns, Boston, and back to the city. Halifax and Saint Johns are in Canada. We don't want no trouble at the border. Get our boy here back home on a Greyhound; there should be one out of Portland."

"Yes, Boss, I'm on it." Brian pulled a phone out of his pocket and typed something into it.

"Dimmie, you take care of old man Kerrick as soon as you find out who he is, and don't make no mess, either. You'll have to wait until the next port to make a clean getaway; it's not like the city where all you gotta do is make a run for it. You run on a ship, *you'll* be swimming with the fishes." Lucky chuckled at his own joke. "You should be able to off the old man the first day, maybe day two."

Eyes wide, Dimmie sputtered, "But, Litt- I mean, Lucky, I don't know nothing about a cruise ship. How'm I even gonna know who he is? I ain't ever seen Mr Kerrick in years. I was just a kid when he…did what he did."

"You saw him the last time any of us saw him. Take this photo. He's an old guy, wears a skinny tie and one of those fedoras like the gangster movies, got a crook in his beak. Just whack him and get off the boat. You'll be gone a couple nights at the most. Meanwhile, get some of that good food I hear about, keep out of trouble, and stay away from the ladies. I'm warning you." Lucky chuckled as Dimmie's ears reddened. "You wouldn't know what to do if you caught one."

Dimmie took the fax Lucky held out to him. He opened his mouth to protest, but Lucky slammed his fist on the desk.

"Let's go, men! Find this old goat before he gets anywhere near that ship. Who does he think he is, coming into my city like he owns the place? Brody, get this fool out of my sight and teach him how to blend in with the swells." Within seconds, the room cleared, leaving only Lucky staring down the hall. Brody had Dimmie by the ear, hauling him like a recalcitrant five-year-old.

Dimmie's the best hitter I got, but the boy has the brains of a sausage. One good thing, he can be counted on to do exactly what he's told. What can possibly go wrong?

Chapter fifteen

Thirty-one hours later, Dimmie grabbed Brody's arm and begged, "Brody, come on, don't make me go! I ain't hardly been out of the 202; how'm I gonna make it on a big fancy cruise ship?"

Brody snapped, "Dimmie, in the name of all that's good and holy, grow up! All you gotta do is rub out one old man. You're going down in history, the boy who took out Colin Kerrick once and for all. You remember now, get off in Portland, leave your stuff behind, and take the 3521 bus. I put the bus tickets in that white envelope in the back pocket of your carry on. Do the job, do it right, like Boss said, and take the Greyhound back to the city. You'll be back before you know it. And hang onto this passport; our man does good work." Brody waved the black sedan to the curb, his voice softening. "Here, take this folder. A nice lady inside the terminal will ask for these papers. Remember what the boss said; just do the job and no thinking. You're not—"

"— very good at it. I know." Dimmie tugged at his collar. "But, Brody, I…"

Joey, the boss' brother, barked at him to get in already and hefted the new suitcase into the trunk. "We ain't got time for this. Traffic is jammed up and we gotta move. Lucky will kill you dead if you miss the boat."

"*Ship,*" Brody sternly corrected. "Dim wit, it's not a boat, you got that?"

At the first red light, Joey glanced at his passenger. Dimmie was sweating so hard, Joey was afraid he would get dehydrated. He lobbed a bottle of water into his lap.

What was the boss thinking, sending the kid on a cruise ship? Dimmie wasn't the sharpest tack on the bulletin board, for sure. In his late twenties, he looked younger. Short for "dim wit" (his own mother called him that), he was well-named. Joey wasn't sure he'd ever heard Dimmie's real name, but the kid was good at taking orders.

Joey waved his fist and navigated around a stalled car while shouting, "Get a horse!" out his window. He knew Dimmie understood what would happen to his mother and grandma if he stepped out of line, after that problem with his two cousins a couple of years ago. Too bad, really; the younger one taught Joey to play poker and always made him laugh, and the other one had those dimples the girls liked. Dimmie was a one-foot-in-front-of-the-other kind of guy. All he had to do was off the old boss, Kerrick. Poor kid was quaking, probably feeling the weight of the whole organization counting on him. Heaven help him if he messed this up.

As the cab idled in traffic on 43rd, Dimmie pulled at the front of his new button up shirt. He could see his heart beating through the stiff fabric. He replayed in his mind Lucky Callahan's last words this morning.

"You look good, real good. I know I can count on you. Just find the old guy and do what you gotta do. Don't do anything else. Don't improvise. Don't do any thinking;

you're no good at it. Just whack old Kerrick and get back here with a report. Same as always. You understand?"

Teeth chattering, Dimmie stammered, "Yes, Boss, I got it, but, Boss, I ain't never been on a ship. How'm I gonna do the job, Boss? Brody said I can't take my Rugar or even my knife with me, the ship has metal detectors, he said. What am I supposed to use, if I can't have my tools?"

"Dimmie, for Pete's sake, you'll figure it out at the time. The main thing is, don't let anybody see you do it, and don't miss the bus back to the city." Lucky handed him his favorite candy from the drawer, a caramel nougat. "Eat this, it'll calm your nerves."

Dimmie stuffed it in his mouth, hearing Mam's voice in his mind. She always said not to eat sticky candy; it made the dentist mad. Dimmie didn't like the dentist. Some days he didn't like Mam, either, always telling him what to do. The Boss was always telling him what to do, too, and he didn't like the way his name sounded when Lucky said it. Like it tasted bad or something.

Sometimes he had to stop and think what his name actually was. The only people who called him by it were the nuns, and most of them stopped after the first few weeks of any school year. Da had named him James-Robert after some king who lived long ago and then died. Dimmie wasn't sure. Da was gone a good long time now. Sometimes Dimmie couldn't remember what his face looked like, but he could still smell Da in his mind, a mixture of boiled cabbage and Marlboros.

Dimmie grabbed the dashboard as the car inched down the line to Pier 88. He cast a last glance at Hell's Kitchen, then squared his shoulders and forced his eyes forward. He blinked, realizing the white hotel in front of him was actually the cruise ship, as tall as some of the smaller buildings in the city. What was it, maybe fifteen or more floors high? Brody said they were called *decks* on a ship, not floors. Rising above the scurry of cars and buses disgorging passengers, the *Ocean Serenity* shone, its flanks lined with balconies, deck chairs at precise angles. He drew a breath, the first full one he'd taken in hours. He'd done a handful of jobs in hotels; he could do this. He had to.

Joey shoved his door open and barked at Dimmie. "Get out already." He grabbed the brand-new suitcase from the trunk and set it on the grimy sidewalk. "Okay, kid, you're on your own. You know what you gotta do. Make us proud. Lucky schmuck, working on a cruise ship!" Without a backward glance, Joey eased the sedan back into traffic, muttering, "And the saints be wit' you."

A bus belched exhaust into the air and Dimmie drew a deep breath, the familiarity calming him. How hard could it be? All he had to do was find the old guy in the photo in his pocket and do what he did best. He wished he had a mug shot instead of a side view taken by a traffic camera. Mug shots were his favorite; a front view and one from the side made it clear who his target was. The police made his job easy sometimes. Other times they got in his way. Some of the younger beat cops were too quick for his liking, showing up just minutes after a job was done, like they were waiting around the corner or something. Like the guy in the bakery shop always said, you gotta take the good with the bad. Life was like that, the man said, and some days were more so than others. Dimmie hoped the next few days wouldn't be the more so kind.

He worried about hitting the wrong guy. He'd seen what happened to Sean last year when he stabbed the wrong target, that Italian politician. Something about diplomatic papers; he didn't remember the details. He wished Sean was here now. If Sean wasn't in the East River, *he'd* be the one to take out Kerrick, and Dimmie would be free to walk the boroughs, where he belonged.

A porter shouted, "Hey, youse goin' or youse gonna stand there all day? Gimme your luggage or get outa my way." He snatched the boarding documents out of Dimmie's hand and swung his suitcase with the other. "Deck five, cabin 507. Cheap seats, but I guess on the boat is better than off the boat, you know what I mean? How much you gonna gimme for a tip, for to make sure your suitcase doesn't end up in Miami or somewheres?"

Dimmie dug in his pocket (extortion, he understood), but the porter laughed and shoved the folder into his hand. "Never mind, take your papers, youse just get on the boat. Bad enough youse is traveling alone. Mind you don't pick up any of them ladies, you know what I mean?" He clapped Dimmie on the shoulder and turned to the next passenger. "Hey, youse goin' or youse gonna stand there all day? Gimme your luggage or get outa my way."

Rubbing his shoulder, Dimmie clutched his black mesh carry on. That's what the clerk at the store called it, a carry on. "Because you gotta *carry it on*, know what I mean?*"* A lot of things had funny names that made no sense, but a carry on for carrying on...Dimmie liked that. The crowd buffeted him, pushing him toward an escalator marked To The Ship. Excited voices swirled around him. A trickle of sweat ran down his neck. How many people were here, anyway? Had to be a couple thou, all pushing toward the ship.

At the top of the escalator, a woman with a fluffy neck scarf reached for the papers in his hand. "Welcome. Little nervous, are we?" Her white teeth parted her too-red lipstick. "No need, you'll love the *Ocean Serenity,* and New England is beautiful this time of year." She pointed him to a line between two ropes. "Check in for the lower decks is over there. Eat a lobster for me." Dimmie nodded, hoping he'd remember. Lobsters he'd seen in the restaurant windows looked like big greenish grey roaches to him, but he didn't want to let the nice lady down.

Chapter sixteen
onboard *Ocean Serenity*

An hour later, Dimmie sat gingerly on a chair by the floor-to-ceiling window. Vertigo washed over him as he peered straight down fourteen decks onto the pier below. He'd felt the same way on a school field trip when the nuns insisted the whole ninth grade go to the top of the Empire State Building, just to say they'd been there. Tourists came from all over the world to see the city from up there, after all. Dimmie liked looking up at the city's tall buildings, but his five story walk up was plenty high for him. The ship's dining room wasn't as high as the Empire State Building, but high enough. Water in the harbor looked almost clean from up here, and his city spiraled on both sides of it like a picture postcard he'd seen in the tourist stores on the Avenues. His foot bumped the carry on on the floor. He'd planned on putting it in his cabin, but hunger drove him to follow his nose to the crowded dining room.

Blinking, he turned his attention back to the menu. Seared Blue Ribeye Sandwich, Cobb Salad, Lime Chicken with Forbidden Rice, Soy Curry Marsala. What is this stuff? His stomach rumbling, he wondered how long he could go without eating. Brody had told him he could have as much food as he wanted on the ship and didn't even have to pay for any of it. It'd be a sweet set up, if only there was any real food to eat.

A little girl called, "Mommy, here's a table! Right here, this man is all alone. Hey, nice man, can me and Mommy sit by you for lunch?"

His eyes lowered, Dimmie bobbed his head.

"If you don't mind...You're not waiting for anyone, are you? Thanks ever so much." A woman slid into the chair across from Dimmie, brushing her long hair behind her. "Sit down, Becky, don't block the waiter. I'm surprised the restaurant is so crowded. Usually on the first day, passengers head to the buffet. I thought only us experienced travelers knew this trick." She held out a slim hand. "I'm Jill, pleased to meet you, and this is my daugh—"

"I'm Becky," the child said, "and Mommy always says I have to say, 'pleased to meet you', but I don't even know you. What's your name?"

Dimmie cleared his throat. "Likewise, I'm sure. My name is Dimmie."

Becky giggled. "That's a funny name."

"Becky, manners! We don't want to hurt Mr Dimmie's feelings, do we? It's probably short for Demetrius, and that's a good, strong Greek name, like your Daddy's."

"No, it's short for James-Robert." The name felt awkward on his lips.

Jill raised a tapered brow. Shrugged. "Even so, Becky, we don't tease people, no matter what. Say you're sorry and we'll order our lunch."

Becky mumbled an apology and Dimmie winked. Her face brightened as the waiter approached.

"I'll take a Lime Chicken, and a cheeseburger for my daughter, please," Jill said, "and bring a fruit plate to share right away. It's hard for her to wait."

Dimmie's stomach rumbled hopefully. "I'll take one of them burgers. No, make it two. And you got any fries? A plate of them, too, while you're at it." He wondered what else there was to eat that nobody put on the fancy menu.

Over lunch, Dimmie's nerves calmed. Becky kept up a steady chatter, saving him from having to say much, and that was fine by him. Jill smiled readily, but he noticed it was the kind of smile that never reached her eyes, as if something was bothering her.

Becky said this was their third cruise. "Daddy's away in the Middle East," she happily reported, "and Mommy says the house gets too empty with just us in it. We're having a girls' getaway. We even packed nail polish with glitter, and Mommy said if I go to sleep right afterwards, I can have cookies and milk for a bedtime snack. Do you know about room service?"

Before Dimmie could get a word in edgewise, Becky explained, "You call the number beside your phone in your cabin and tell them what you want to eat, and somebody brings it right to you, even if you're in your *pajamas*!"

Dimmie hoped his cabin had a phone with the number by it; it sounded less risky than eating meals in the dining room where he had to mind his manners the whole time. If he could order a slice or a foot long, this cruise might just turn out all right. But first, he had to find old man Kerrick. Orders were orders. He glanced around the vast dining room. If he could spot Kerrick right off, he'd be able to make a plan to off the old guy. He patted his pocket, missing the weight of his blade.

"What's that?" he asked. "Say again."

"I said, I'm sure you've been on loads of cruises, but if you're not familiar with the ship, you might look into a ship's tour. It'll be on your daily program." Jill stood and extended her cool hand. "We're going to unpack. Pleasure to meet you. See you around."

"And get ice cream, too, Mommy, you promised. Bye, Mr Dimmie!" With a jaunty wave, Becky took her mother's hand and they headed toward the exit without even paying their tab.

"Sweet deal," Dimmie muttered. He pushed back his chair and picked his teeth. What would it be like to have a girl like Becky, a daughter of his own? Not to mention a wife as pretty as that Jill, even if she did seem a little sad under the surface. Lucky wasn't big on his boys getting married. He said if mobsters were meant to have a family of their own, they'd have been born with one. It wasn't like back when Mr Kerrick was in charge. Kerrick said a wife was good for calming a man's nerves. Maybe that's what Lucky needed. He sure wasn't calm.

The agent at check in said to read the daily program to find out what was going on. Dimmie wasn't much for reading, but with Jill saying it, too, he'd better look at it. Mam was a big believer in omens, and he didn't want to miss any of them. A tour of the ship would be the best way to find his way around before sail away. *Sail away;* sounded like one of those fancy dance clubs in mid-town. Brody told him to blend in, and if sail away is what the toffs did, count him in.

Chapter seventeen

Dimmie reviewed the plan in his mind, the back of his neck knotting up again. Get onboard, check out the ship, blend in, find the lay of the place. Sea day tomorrow, when the ship just sailed nowhere. He was supposed to walk around the ship until he spotted Kerrick. Once he found him, he should find out where his cabin is and be ready to follow him off the ship when they docked in Bar Harbor the following morning. Track him and rub him out when the chance arose, and don't make a scene, that's what Brody said. Killing a man in rival territory was risky; Lucky said if he didn't feel good about it, to just kill him on the ship, maybe after the ship left Bar Harbor. Either way, he was to lay low and act normal until the time came.

It'd be easier to act normal if anything was familiar. Maybe the ship's tour would help. And maybe he'd spot the place the little girl talked about. Ice cream always settled his stomach. Gelato, too. What flavors would a ship have?

Bar Harbor was a small town with plenty of places to kill a man, Brody said, and nobody owned the turf. Lucky disagreed, said that wouldn't work for a hit; no good hiding spots, Dimmie guessed. Lucky's IT man had found out Kerrick had a tour booked through the ship all day. Dimmie didn't know why he was called "Eye Tee Man." Everybody had a name, didn't they? Eye Tee must be short for something; a lot of the guys had nicknames.

The Bar Harbor Acadia Park tour was full—Eye Tee Guy had grabbed the last ticket— and there might not be a chance for Dimmie to get the old guy alone. If he didn't see a good opportunity during the day, he'd get back onboard and do the deed that night. The ship would stop in Portland the day after Bar Harbor. That's where Dimmie was to get off and take a Greyhound back to the city while the ship sailed on to Halifax, Nova Scotia and Saint Johns, New Brunswick, then back to Boston and New York. Colin Kerrick had to be rubbed out by the time they reached Canada. And Dimmie didn't want to stay onboard any longer than he had to.

Last night, after the store closed, a sales clerk had picked out suitable clothing and made Dimmie try them on, then come out and show off for Brody, one after another, like a mannequin. Like one of those models in the fashion district, only not so skinny. Did those women ever eat? He was pretty sure his skeleton was fatter than their whole body. Looked like a stiff wind would blow them away. He saw them sometimes, two or three together, on the subway or walking through a park. He'd never seen one of them smile. Maybe their faces were too tight for that. Maybe they'd feel happier if they had a good meal.

In between trips to the dressing room, Brody had gone over and over the plan until he was sure Dimmie had it clear in his mind. Dimmie asked about those funny-sounding places after Portland. Brody shook his head and told him forget about it. Those places were in Canada, a whole foreign country, and anyway, Dimmie was to get off the ship long before then, did he understand?

Dimmie didn't know about Nova Scotia or New Brunswick, but he had a bad feeling about that other place on the list, Halifax. A couple of years after what Kerrick did, Dimmie had a run in with Big Harry's man near Times Square. Dimmie saw the guy push over an old lady with a walker, somebody's grandma, just for the heck of it, then laugh. Dimmie followed him and slashed his tires while he was in a restaurant. Sitting in the front window to keep an eye on the car like Lucky's men did, Harry's bodyguard made him as Dimmie walked away. He didn't care; you don't knock over old ladies for no good reason.

Later that night, walking down 33rd, somebody bumped into Dimmie and slipped him a note. "We know what you did. Avoid Halifax if you like breathing." Dimmie did, indeed, like breathing, and made up his mind to not leave the boroughs if he could help it.

He couldn't remember if he'd ever been out of the 202; he hardly went farther than the neighborhood. Mam said Da took him all the way to Philly one time, but he was too young to remember. Most days, he could barely remember Da's face, either. It looked like a watery photograph in his mind. He never told Mam. She talked about him every day like he was still there, like maybe he'd run out for a pack and was going to come back any time now. Da used to like to go new places, but Mam didn't, so Dimmie and Gran didn't go anywhere, either.

Now he had to go all the way to Portland, Maine, on a boat that moved. Like the Staten Island Ferry, he figured, only bigger. He didn't mind the ferry. He liked watching the faces of the people seeing the Statue of Liberty that close, some for the first time. They liked to pose for pictures by the railing. Some took those selfies to send to their friends. A couple of times, a tourist asked him to take their photo, so everybody could be in it at once. Dimmie was careful to hold their camera real still and he always took three shots. One was bound to turn out good if he took a couple of extras, he figured, and not catch somebody with their eyes closed or mouth open or talking. Even if somebody was saying something nice, like "watermelon," they still looked goofy in a picture. Mam kept her pictures in a shoebox, and there were a lot with people either talking or eating. Eating made people's faces look funny, too. Stretched out-like.

The cruise ship was a whole lot bigger than the Staten Island Ferry, and this boat even had bedrooms. No, it was a ship; Brody said not to call it a boat. And *cabins*, not bedrooms. At least it wouldn't pitch and roll like the ferry; that's what the lady at the check-in desk said. In a storm, the ferry felt like one of those bathtub toys he played with when he was a kid, until Mam threw them all away when he turned eighteen. The ship was still tied to the dock, so he didn't know. He hoped the lady was telling the truth.

He skimmed the daily program given him at check in, then gave up. Too many words. On his way out of the dining room, he asked the white-coated bellhop by the door if he knew where the ship tour started. *Up two decks, midships, wait by the purser's, ten minutes.* Taking pity on Dimmie's blank face, a nearby crew member smiled and said she was going to Guest Services in the same area and he could walk with her.

Dimmie tried to follow the woman's chatter as they walked past artwork and up the crowded staircase, dodging passengers with those rolling suitcases. They looked as lost as he felt. He'd never seen so much glass and brass in one place, fancier even than the upscale hotels on Times Square. Not that he'd spent a lot of time in those; a couple of jobs was all.

"Elevators are jammed on embarkation day. Just wait until we get to Halifax," she said. "This is nothing. Passengers line up hours early just to get the first tender. First cruise? You'll love it." She nudged his arm. "Let's cut through this hatch. They're still bunkering on the starboard rail, so the prom deck is closed for now. Don't worry, the barge will be out of the way in time for the sail away soiree."

Swah ray? Why didn't people speak English here? Baffled, Dimmie followed the woman. A prom deck? He'd skipped the prom his senior year. Dates were required and he saved himself the pain of being turned down by just not asking a girl. Mam had thrown a fit when she learned he wasn't going, but Mam wasn't on this cruise and he could do as he pleased. Nobody could make him go.

Dimmie ran his hand over his cropped hair, marveling at the bronze and blown-glass décor of the ship. That sculpture alone had to be worth a few hundred thou. Had Little Boss ever considered lifting some of it? There was plenty; they wouldn't miss a few pieces. Anybody could just take it.

Hit men don't do art theft.

Lucky Callahan kept the lines of the organization clear. Maybe he could tell the boss about it when he got home again. All he had to do was blend in now, find Kerrick and take him out when he found an opportunity. That's what hitmen do, not stealing art. But who'd notice if a couple of small pieces found their way into his luggage? He knew how to evade security cameras. How else would have stayed alive this long?

Chapter eighteen

The long corridor opened into a wide foyer. Dimmie craned his head back, counting the glossy railings reaching upward. He stopped at ten; no need to strain his eyes, after all. Passengers gathered in small groups, chattering like the magpie documentary he saw last month.

The crew member touched Dimmie's arm and he recoiled. With a raised eyebrow, she said, "Here you go, Sir, wait right over here. Jackie's leading the tour. She'll be here any minute." With a smile, she assured him, "And don't be nervous; you're going to have a great cruise."

Dimmie sank into a blue plush sofa against a wall. Its rounded back reminded him of the ones in the lobby of the Grand Biloxi Hotel in Midtown, where he'd staked out that gambler from Jersey last year. The guys should have known better than to run a high-stakes poker game without asking the boss first. You don't just set up shop outside your turf; everyone knew that. He hadn't enjoyed the hit—he never did—but the hotel was over the top gorgeous.

Chilled, Dimmie wondered who owned the ship. The E3-4s, the Russians, Asians, maybe? Why hadn't Brody given him more details? He didn't like rush jobs. He kept his back to the wall, scanning the passengers. A few pressed closer, holding the daily schedule. They must be here for the tour, too. Didn't anybody hold still?

A minute later, a young woman wearing a green Staff shirt approached the sofa. "Welcome aboard, everybody! I'm Jackie, and I'm going to show you all around the ship. We'll go to the Playbill Theatre first. Walk this way, please."

A handful of passengers followed her. Dimmie was careful to bring up the rear. His hand felt for the comfort of the small Rugar LCP custom he carried in his pocket. He gulped, remembering he'd had to leave it in his sock drawer, pocket holster and all.

"No guns on cruise ships," Brody had insisted. Easy for him to say. He wasn't the one sent to kill the old boss on a cruise ship not even attached to land. Brody was nothing but a paper-pusher, when it came down to it.

Dimmie wondered why he couldn't have his pistol. It fit in his hand; who'd even notice? He took his little pistol lots of places labeled No Gun zones, but Brody was adamant. When Dimmie asked how was he supposed to take care of the old guy without his favorite piece, Brody punched the wall. "Geeze, do I gotta tell you everything? Figure it out at the time, dummy!"

"Dimmie, I'm *Dimmie,* not dummy," Dimmie mumbled. He'd left the gun home, as ordered, but he felt as off-kilter as that day last week when he put his boxers on backwards. It was lunchtime before he had a chance to turn them around.

How to kill Kerrick had been on his mind pretty much every waking moment. Without his tools, this job was anything but routine. Somebody in the boarding area had joked about throwing his buddy overboard, waiting

five minutes, then yelling Man Overboard. Dimmie took
note; that was a good idea. A ship this size couldn't exactly
turn on a dime. And it wasn't likely the old boss could
swim, either.

Now that he'd seen how tall the ship's railings
were, Dimmie wasn't sure he could lob a guy over the side
without him making a fuss on the way down. It depended
on how big old Kerrick was these days, too. Old men tend
to shrink, like the tobacco shop owner down from their
apartment. Back when Dimmie was only ten years old, he
could already see over the man's head, but the old boss was
taller than that. Some of the old men he'd seen getting
onboard looked like they could be knocked over by a stiff
wind. Was Kerrick like that? He could always bash the old
guy's head in, but Dimmie didn't like seeing what was
inside somebody's head. It made his stomach feel funny,
like the time he ate four hot dogs on the street, and threw
them up right on Ninth Avenue. Maybe he could—

"Oh, so sorry! I guess I stopped too suddenly." A
woman in her twenties giggled and batted her eyelashes at
Dimmie. Her voice sounded like those crooners on the
street outside the clubs.

Flustered, Dimmie had never seen lashes that long.
They looked like black spiders folded in half. Mumbling an
apology for bumping into her, his face burned. Jackie was
saying something about production shows and how many
people the theater could seat. Blood pounded in Dimmie's
ears, drowning her words.

An unbidden thought washed over him.

I'm alone. No one knows me. If I wanna take in a show like the swells, I can do it and nobody can tell me different.

Smiling at the young woman, he realized he could do anything, be anybody, on the ship. He could even talk to the ladies, and no one would know. Brody said over and over again he was to blend in, act like anybody else. So long as he got rid of Colin Kerrick and took the 3521 Greyhound express back to the city, who was to know? His shoulders, which had been up around his ears, relaxed. He scanned the theatre—so much bronze and velvet! — and followed the group led by Jackie down a long hall.

She said the casino would be closed the entire cruise due to the shoreline proximity, whatever that meant. Lucky never let his boys gamble, of course, but Dimmie thought he'd picked up enough tips to be pretty good at poker, maybe even blackjack. Now he wouldn't get to even try. But he would definitely take in a show.

Jackie led the group to the two-level dining room, where Dimmie had eaten lunch with that nice woman and her little girl. She introduced a man in a white dinner jacket with some French name. May Tree Dee or something. Dimmie stood back while the other passengers oohed and ahhed over the elegant venue. A couple complained about not liking their table, and the lah-tee-dah man promised to make it right. Dimmie frowned. What could be wrong with a table, so long as it had food on it? If there was anything to complain about, it was the menu with those fancy words and the good stuff not even listed.

Jackie said they'd be going up to the pool deck, with a few stops along the way. As they walked through the ship, Dimmie sidestepped passengers and kept an eye out for places where an old guy like Kerrick might hang out. Too bad the casino was closed. That would have been a good place to look for old man. He'd been pretty good back in the day, Dimmie'd heard.

Dimmie wished he'd had more time to learn about Kerrick. Usually, he studied his mark for days before a hit. He barely knew Kerrick and was certain the old man wouldn't remember him. Dimmie had only been in the room a time or two when Kerrick was the Big Boss, before the bad thing happened and Lucky Callahan moved up in the ranks to become the boss. Back when Lucky was just a second-hand man and Kerrick was in charge, Dimmie was a kid, a go-fer, running errands and holding doors open, never making eye contact with the higher-ups.

That was before somebody took Dimmie to a shooting range as a joke and found out he could hit a receipt at three hundred yards.

The one thing he remembered about Kerrick was his voice, a mixture of music and gravel, a kind of sing-song that'd flatten your tires and make you smile about it. And his smell; peppermint and Old Spice. The guy must have bathed in Old Spice, like older men did back in the day. Kerrick kept peppermints in his pocket, the hard white kind that went to dust when you bit into it. Peppermints; the boys said Kerrick had passed them out like candy. They said other things, too, when Lucky wasn't around. Why hadn't Dimmie paid more attention?

What if he couldn't recognize Kerrick? A lot of years had passed. Brody said he couldn't take the photo with him, the one the Eye Tee guy printed from a fax machine. Brody said he had to look at it and make it stick in his mind. Brody said a lot of things, but he wasn't the one who had to take out a stranger on a cruise ship full of people. Dimmie strained to recall the grainy image, a side view of a guy with one of those old-man hats half pulled down his face. How did Little Boss even know it was him on the One train?

"There you go, thinking again," Lucky's voice rang in his mind. *"Don't ever think, Dimmie. You're no good at it. Just do as you're told and nothing else, you hear me?"*

"Yes, B—" Dimmie caught himself. Jackie was saying something about the library, where quieter passengers gathered to read the newspapers and do crosswords. A memory surfaced; Colin Kerrick setting aside a newspaper opened to the crossword puzzle on his desk, telling Sean to settle with a crew of Filipinos. Said he thought were smuggling those kind of women into the City. Dimmie to this day didn't know what kind of women Colin was talking about.

He wished he'd been listening; where else had Jackie said an old guy might hang out?

"Last stop on our tour is deck sixteen, the pool deck, where all the action takes place. Live music four times a day. Right after muster drill, join us there for the best sail away party at sea." She held the elevator door open while the group jockeyed for space.

Dimmie held back, letting the rest of the group go on ahead of him. "I can't, I gotta—" he blurted. With one memory of Boss Kerrick fresh in his mind, he needed to find a quiet place to see if any more would bubble up. Peppermint. Old Spice. Crosswords.

Jackie smiled indulgently. "No problem, Sir, go down the corridor to your left. Use the men's room is past the planter." The elevator door slid closed.

Dimmie headed for the men's room, eying the flower pot. Who knew flowers grew on ships? Once inside, he wondered why Jackie had sent him here. Not wanting to waste the trip, he washed his hands, humming *Yankee Doodle* under his breath. Mam taught him that's how long to hold his hands under the water. Just dipping and drying didn't cut it with her. Brody had reminded him a dozen times or more to wash his hands every time he was near a men's room, even if he hadn't touched anything. He said there was something bad on cruise ships, something called Noro, that could make a man so sick, he wouldn't care if he lived or died. Dimmie liked being alive, and besides, he hadn't even seen his cabin yet.

He turned around twice, but saw no paper towel dispenser. What kind of place was this, with no paper towels? Maybe the ship decided adding more mirrors was more important than leaving room for a paper towel holder. Not wanting to streak the leg of his new pants, he dried his hands on a soft towel, one of a stack neatly rolled on the counter. Once it was damp and wrinkled, he couldn't put it back. He stuffed it in his pocket for later. You never know when you might need one. If worse came to worst, a washcloth made a decent gag.

A voice came over the loudspeaker. The staterooms were now available for passengers' use. Dimmie wasn't clear on if the Eye Tee guy had booked a stateroom or a cabin, but he knew he was to stay in number 507. He consulted a bronze map by the elevator. Up a couple of decks, turn left, halfway down the hallway.

The elevator door slid open, and he stepped in, followed by two women in those motorized scooters old ladies used. Pushed to the back of the elevator, he felt a familiar wave of vertigo. The inside walls of the elevator were glass, floor to ceiling, and his stomach turned over.

"I gotta get out—" Red-faced, Dimmie half-climbed over the scooters, over the ladies, over the young family that pushed inside after him, blocking the door with an arm before it closed. He heard grumbles as the door slid closed, but his feet were on solid ground and that mattered more than manners, no matter what Mam said.

Chapter nineteen

Dimmie headed for the carpeted staircase to the left. A handful of people came down and he waited for them, before trudging up the stairs, counting the decks as he went. Each landing had a huge painting, worth a pretty penny, he was sure. By deck eight, his lungs burned. What all had Brody put in his carry on, anyway?

He finally reached his deck and peeled off the stairs. The painting here was of a herd of elephants with their babies; Dimmie was mindful of landmarks, and what was cuter than baby animals? He dug the key card out of his pocket and slipped it in the lock, just like at the hotels, only this card was his, not one he'd filched from a maid's cleaning cart. He swung open the door to his cabin and yelped. A man about his age gasped and dropped the ice bucket in his hands.

"Who are you and what are you doing in here?" Dimmie growled, his hand on the doorknob. The space wasn't big enough for a fight, but he could clock the guy one if he had to.

The cabin steward offered his hand and a shaky smile. "Emil, at your service. Sorry to startle you. I was merely preparing your room." He dropped to his knees, scooping ice cubes into the waste basket.

Dimmie knelt to help; Mam always told him to be a good boy. At Emil's protest, Dimmie sat back on his heels. "You work here?"

"Yes, sir, I'm your steward. Welcome aboard. If you need anything—"

"I don't need nothing. On second thought, Stu, I'm not in the mood for a hoity-toity supper, at least not yet, but I'm getting hungry. You know of a place on this boat where I can get a meal without putting on the fancy togs I got in my suitcase?"

"It's Emil, Sir, not Stu. I understand; after a long day of travel, the main dining room may not suit. May I suggest the buffet on deck fourteen? Casual dining, and a good selection."Emil stood. "Most people prefer the aft elevators, the glass ones, but once you've seen them, I suggest the midship ones, which tend to be less crowded. Also, I took the liberty of unpacking your things."

Dimmie's heart thumped; good thing he hadn't packed his blade or Rugar against Brody's orders. "You unpacked for me?"

"Yes, the luggage was delivered early. I slid your suitcase under the bed. How else may I serve you, Mr James-Robert?"

"I guess I got the rest." It had been a long time since anybody called him by his given name. "And don't feel bad about spilling the ice, Stu." Dimmie hustled the steward out of the room.

Dimmie set his carry on in the narrow closet and flexed his arms. The cabin was small, smaller than the few hotel rooms he'd had hits in, but it was all his. The cabin had a big bed, all to himself. He turned on every light, then bounced once on the bed (Mam didn't tolerate bed-bouncing) and opened the bathroom door. It smelled fresh, not like the ones in the apartments in the city. He sniffed the paper-wrapped soap bar. No one to share or leave wet hair stuck into it like the one in the shower at home. Ahh.

And that Stu was all right; he even told him how to avoid those glass elevators without being asked. Maybe if he saw him again, he could ask about that phone number little Becky mentioned for room service.

Chapter twenty

His stomach grumbled. Deck fourteen, the steward told him. As he walked down the long corridor toward the midship elevator, Dimmie considered. He was supposed to be working. Lucky said to find old man Kerrick first thing, but he was hungry. Anyway, it wasn't like the vic could make a run for it, what with the ship moving and not stopping until the day after tomorrow. Better to get his bearings, find the old boss man, then figure out a plan.

Besides, old people like buffets, right? Like the old-time cafeterias in the neighborhood, until the new places called eateries took over their corners. With any luck, he might spot Kerrick having a snack. Patting his wallet, he followed a family into the buffet, his mouth watering at the tempting aromas coming from beautifully arrayed stations.

Nothing like Saint Margaret's school cafeteria, where you could get anything you wanted, so long as you wanted mystery meat with grey sauce and gummy mashed potatoes four days a week. On Fridays, they served watery fish stew. The peas in the stew were a sickly grey-green, and they floated. Josie joked every Friday, "They're the color of a dead leprechaun," but he'd never seen a leprechaun, dead or alive, so he didn't know. He did know the fish stew turned his stomach, the stench increasing throughout the morning, filling the halls and classrooms with a greasy dead-fish odor until lunchtime, when he came face to face with it.

And woe to anybody who didn't eat every drop of it. A kid could plan on a smack from Sister's ruler, and a lecture on the evils of wasting food provided by the Good Lord Above, followed by a trip to the Reverend Mother's office, if there was any backtalk. He often wondered why the Good Lord Above, who the nuns said provided all things and created the rest, couldn't pony up fresh fish, just once, for the students at Saint Margaret's. He never asked; he spent enough time in the Reverend Mother's office as it was.

A white-coated woman greeted Dimmie and handed him a chilled plate. "Welcome aboard. Here you go, Sir, for the salad bar. Heated plates are over by the hot station."

"How much chow can I have?"

"As much as you like, sir, and you can come back for more."

"And do I pay now or after I eat?" Brody had told him the food was free, but who'd be stupid enough to fall for that?

Dimples bloomed beside her smile. "No charge. It's complementary, Sir, part of the cruise fare. Try the chicken salad with pistachios. Everyone raves about it."

Dimmie bobbed his head and moved to the line, plate in hand, wondering what a pistachio was and who was supposed to compliment who. Big bowls of bright salads and chilled vegetables, free for the taking, next to big bowls of whole shrimp and glossy pink morsels in little black seashells. Sweet deal. He glanced across the way, where a white-jacketed man with a broad smile carved slices of roast beef with a long knife, forking them onto passenger's plates. Mam insisted he eat his vegetables before he touched meat, but he'd have some of that beef before he left the cafeteria. *Buffet*, the sign by the door said. He spooned garlicky green beans and fried potatoes onto his plate next to a slab of ham, and added a crusty roll.

A little while later, Dimmie sat back, loosening his belt a notch. Turns out pistachios were hard little nuts, and the beef was as good as it looked. A waiter who kept his lemonade glass full suggested he try the pavlova for dessert. Another new word, but Dimmie was game.

Luckily, the dessert array had little signs telling what each item was, same as the rest of the foods. He wouldn't have guessed the little white cloud-puffs were pavlova. Pavlova sounded like something more solid, maybe like Mam's stale-bread pudding. Turns out, they were airy and sweet, melting on his tongue, cream topped with a red berry and a slice of something tart, green with black seeds. He stood and crossed the buffet to the dessert display and took two more from the platter.

He surveyed the room as he headed back to his table. Passengers ate, chattering, moving to fill their plates, sitting alone or in groups. Over by the big windows, a couple of tables held card-players, but he couldn't see what game they were playing from that distance. He skimmed each face as he slowly returned to his table. Little Becky waved to him from a table by the post, then said something to her mother, and Jill waved with a broad smile. He smiled back; a familiar face never hurt, and after not seeing a soul he knew since he'd come on the ship, Becky and Jill made his heart warm.

Dimmie kept the image of old Colin Kerrick in his mind, but none of the men in the buffet looked anything like him. Wait—was that him, sitting by the woman in the orange top? Dimmie set his pavlova plate on his table and moved closer, taking care to keep a large man walking to his seat between him and the old man. What were the chances of Kerrick recognizing Dimmie after all these years? Just as the big man pulled back his chair, the old man stood with his hand on the orange-bloused woman's arm.

Unless he'd had that plastic surgery Dimmie'd heard about in the last two days, that wasn't Colin Kerrick. Not with a nose that straight. And Lucky hadn't said anything about a woman with him. Dimmie tried to remember; the old boss was married, but what did Mrs Boss look like? He returned to his table.

The waiter apologized, "I'm so sorry, Sir, I thought you had finished your meal. Please, let me bring you another dessert." Sighing at the empty table, Dimmie said, "No, forget about it. I got work to do." The pleasure supper had brought him faded.

Lucky sent him here to do a job, not to fill his gut.

Determined to find the old mob boss, Dimmie decided to look in every place he could see where an old man might be on the ship. People swirled like on 43rdAve at noon, and the ship had plenty of places for one old gusto hide. For all he knew, Kerrick could be holed up in his cabin, avoiding the public areas of the ship.

On the other hand, what did Kerrick have to hide from? He had no idea Lucky Callahan wanted him dead, no idea Dimmie was on a mission. Dimmie wondered what the old man was thinking, coming back to the city after so long. If he had a chance, before he killed Kerrick, maybe he'd ask him. Sean used to talk with his vics before he killed them. Dimmie never had, but maybe this time he'd start. Mam always said it never hurts to be friendly.

Meanwhile, the night was young, as Lucky often said, and with so many passengers moving about the ship, Dimmie could walk around and narrow down where the old boss might be.

Too bad the casino was closed; that would be an obvious place for the old mob boss to hang out. He'd heard Kerrick played a mean game of five-card stud, and his blackjack skill was still talked about, but never when Lucky was around.

Old habits die hard, he'd heard, but what habits did Kerrick have besides poker and running the ponies? He'd heard he had a fondness for the dancers on Broadway, and bought season tickets for the Rockettes. That must have been hard to give up when he went into witness protection. The billboards advertising the shows looked terrific, and that poster by Rockefeller Square—! He'd never met a real woman with legs that long.

He walked down to the atrium, they called it, like a hotel lobby, and stood with his back to a wall, watching passengers swarm. They all looked like they had somewhere to be, all but him. A back-lit poster caught Dimmie's eye. A production show, eight o'clock, in the theater on deck six and seven. He wasn't sure what a production was, other than Lucky kept telling him not to make one when he complained, but the theater was a logical place to look for the old mob boss. Plus, he'd made up his mind to go to a show.

Dimmie patted his wallet again. No ticket prices were listed, but he had the cash Brody had given him to use for "incidentals," whatever that meant. Seven forty-three; he had time to make the show, if it wasn't sold out. He hurried up one flight of stairs and through a bar and joined a slow-moving herd of passengers trailing up a carpeted ramp into the theater. Passing heavy maroon velvet curtains, he didn't see a ticket booth, or ticket takers like they had at the movies, either. He slipped in. If anybody made him pay, he could just say he hadn't seen any ticket taker. Which was true.

Awed by the brass and velvet seats, he forgot all about looking for Kerrick. He spotted an empty seat down front, middle section, headed for it, and no one said a word to stop him. He waited in the aisle until a barman handed a woman a colorful drink, then brushed past her and settled into a plush seat on row four, marveling at the curtain onstage. Lights played on the sequined...what was that, anyway? Some kind of a bird with a long plumed tail, sewn right onto the curtain itself. Who knew such a thing existed?

Voices swirled around him, quieting abruptly at a thunder of drums. He grinned as the house lights lowered and the curtain swept open, revealing twelve dancers in bright costumes. Nearly as good as the Rockettes, he figured, and just as pretty. The music swelled, the dancers paraded their feathers, and Dimmie applauded so hard, his hands smarted. A man could get used to this.

As the house lights came on at the end of the show, he rose, waiting for others to make their way up the aisle to the exits. He stared up at the balcony. From up there, he'd have a view of everybody below, and maybe he could find Colin Kerrick. He'd stake out a seat up there another night. The sooner he found him, the sooner he could do the job and quit thinking about it. He liked having his mind clear.

He glanced reluctantly at the shimmering curtain, now closed. What else had he missed? All those years growing up mere blocks from Broadway, yet he'd never been to a live performance. Mam told him years ago they were for tourists who were no better than they ought to be, not god-fearing people who were raised to know better.

Mam wasn't on the ship, and Dimmie pushed back the rising guilt. He hadn't thought much about God in his life, and wasn't sure what he had to fear about Him, anyway. What was so bad about watching people singing and dancing, even if their costumes were kind of skimpy? Better than what the ladies wore at the clubs on 33rd. Now *those* were some long legs. Mam would beat him with her skillet if she knew he'd ever set foot in there. Some things, she was better off not knowing. Life was hard enough.

While the crowd slowly emptied the theater, he edged left toward a spiral staircase. He clung to the railing, never having seen steps like these, and climbed to the balcony level. The seats below were nearly all empty, the last stragglers heading for the aisle. He stood in the aisle, watching passengers below exiting the theatre. Quite a few old men were onboard, from what he could tell. Colin Kerrick could be any of them.

Lucky saw the old boss getting on the One train, but he didn't say anything about him walking with a cane; that eliminated some of the passengers. Dimmie tried to narrow it down further. Digging deep in his memory, he strained to recall what old man Kerrick's wife looked like. Faint memories surfaced as if out of a fog bank. Red-headed, wasn't she? He'd only heard Mrs Kerrick speak once or twice, with a voice that reminded him of tinkling bells at Christmas. Well, that was a long time ago; she could have let her hair go grey. Maybe she even died.

But would an old man go on a cruise alone? On the other hand, Dimmie was alone, and he'd overheard those girls in the elevator saying they were alone, too, on a break from college. College was a place as foreign as Jupiter. Mam and Gran both demanded he finish high school, but Dimmie'd been so glad to finally leave Saint Margaret's behind, they couldn't have paid him to go to school for another day. Of course, no one tried.

From his bird's-nest vantage point, Dimmie had a view of almost every seat below. If Colin Kerrick attended a show, he'd spot him for certain. He made up his mind to attend tomorrow's show—some man who called himself a Cruise Director said everybody should not miss it. Mam would never know, and there was nobody to tell her.

Dimmie stretched. He'd heard some passengers talking about a midnight buffet tonight. Mam always said he had a hollow left leg, and while Dimmie wondered how she knew that, he was more tired than hungry. He took an elevator—the solid one, not the glass-walled one—to deck five and slid his key card into the door lock.

A bear made of towels stood on his bed, with chocolates for eyes. Mesmerized, Dimmie turned it over and over in his hands. He unwrapped a candy left on the turned-down bed. That Stu knew how to make a man feel taken care of. Dimmie locked the door and settled into bed without even brushing his teeth. No reason to spoil the taste of chocolate.

Chapter twenty-one

Dimmie wasn't one for a big breakfast, although Mam always said it set the tone for the whole day. On a cruise ship with soft music playing nearly everywhere Dimmie went, he figured the day already had enough tone on its own. He wanted to breathe some sea air. It smelled different than in the city. Gone were the pervasive odors of exhaust, various cooking foods, and body odor. Standing by the railing on deck six—the Promenade, a sign said—Dimmie watched the wake lapping at the side of the ship.

A solitary sea bird dove at the waves, but other than that, the horizon was as empty as anything he'd ever seen. Not a single building or vehicle, just endless water stretching to a hazy grey line. Vertigo washed over him; so much nothingness! Why had the Good Lord Above squashed so many people into the city, when there was so much extra space on earth? Well, he wasn't a fish; that explained it. He noticed a log bobbing on the waves.

A few feet away, a child exclaimed, "Mama! I see a mermaid!"

Dimmie edged closer, trying to see what the boy was pointing at, but all he saw was the log. On closer look, he made out a face. *A real mermaid!* Wait'll he told Lucky and Brody. Nah; they'd only laugh at him.

"Honey, that's just a harbor seal," a woman nearby said. "Watch, it'll probably duck under the water soon."

Sure enough, it rolled over and dove beneath the waves. Dimmie's heart pounded. A real live harbor seal, like on the Nature channel! Almost as good as a mermaid. He watched another minute or two, hoping the creature would surface. How long could it hold its breath, anyway? He gave up and headed for the coffee shop he'd passed on his way out onto the open deck.

Taking his place at the end of the line, he stared at the menu board. Chai tea, espresso, latte, Americano, cappuccino. He wasn't sure how to say those names right and didn't want to risk the server laughing at him. He heard that enough at home, but how was a guy to know? When his turn came, he pointed at the cream-filled pastry in the glass case and asked for one of those powdered sugar donuts, too.

"And to drink, Sir?" the woman smiled, making eye contact. He'd never seen anybody with eyes that color. Green-blue, like the gems Brody poured on Lucky's desk after that heist last month. Mobsters didn't steal artwork, but Luck made an exception for jewelry, Dimmie guessed. Or maybe the take fell into his lap. Dimmie never had anything good fall into *his* lap, but that's what Lucky said sometimes.

He sputtered, but no words came out. Those *eyes!*

"Sir? Did you say hot tea?"

"Haa…ah…" Words failed.

"Certainly, one hot cocoa coming up." With a nod, the woman turned. A minute later, she presented Dimmie with a steaming cup and a broad smile. "Extra cream, one jelly donut, one pastry horn. They just came out. Enjoy."

Dimmie carried the cup and plate to a corner table. Boss always said to choose a table with your back to the wall, so's nobody could come up behind you. Dimmie felt no threat from the milling passengers, but there sure were a lot of them. He wiped his brow with a paper napkin and glanced at the woman behind the counter. Those *eyes.*

Lucky's voice rang in his ears. "Leave the ladies alone. You wouldn't know what to do with one."

Maybe it was time he found out. He wasn't a kid anymore.

Sipping his hot cocoa, Dimmie skimmed the daily program Stu had placed on his bed last night. Dimmie wasn't much for reading books, but Brody told him he'd better read every paper he found on the ship. He didn't expect anything about old Colin Kerrick to be in the daily program, but Dimmie followed orders and read it, every word.

Acupuncture seminar, foot analysis, art auction, Bingo, aft pool open 9am-10pm, shuffleboard on deck four…How was a person supposed to know what all those words meant? Acupuncture, he recognized from that sign near his apartment at home. Sean told him it meant somebody sticking needles into you to make you feel better, but Dimmie didn't believe a word of it.

Wiping the last of the powdered sugar from his hands, he walked out onto the open Promenade. A gust of cool fresh air made him take a deep breath. The ocean sure smelled different than the city streets. If he lingered in one place long enough, maybe Colin Kerrick would walk right by. For all he knew old Colin could be walking the ship, too, five minutes behind him. He'd heard if a person stood still in Midtown long enough, the whole city would pass by him. Did that work on cruise ships?

The fresh breeze rippled his hair. A handful of passengers gathered on the open deck, near some painted lines on the floor. Dimmie moved closer; had they spotted another seal in the water?

A crew member came up behind him and took Dimmie's arm. "Here's our last team member!"She hissed, "You don't mind, do you, Sir, making the teams come out even? We can't start without even numbers."

"Mr Dimmie! Over here, come be on my team with Mommy and me!" Becky pulled at his other arm, her pigtails bouncing.

Dimmie nodded at Jill. "I...I...I don't know—"

Jill smiled warmly. "No problem. Shuffleboard is easy. Here; take a couple of practice shots while they're writing down team names. You just line the weight up like this and give the cue a good shove. Try to get the disc in the numbered sections on the board down there." Jill showed him how to hold the cue, which was nothing like the cues he used for playing pool. He pushed the little biscuit-thing with the stick, and watched it slide down the painted board on the floor. It stopped on ten.

Becky cheered. "Mr Dimmie, you're a natch at this! We'll win for sure with you on our team."

Dimmie's heart thudded against his shirt. Pressure—what if it was just a lucky shot? This wasn't anything like shooting. The staff member arranged the teams, making notes on her clip board. Wiping sweat from his forehead, Dimmie took his turns, closing his eyes as he pushed the puck. Another ten, a nine, two sevens, two more tens.

Becky danced and cheered with every shot, her ruffled skirt dancing along with her. Jill encouraged him. "Are you sure you never played before? You're really good!" Dimmie's face warmed at the unfamiliar praise. At the end of the game, he grinned and accepted one of the ceramic mugs, prizes for each of the winning team members. Second place team received ship-logo pens. The teams high-fived, agreeing to meet for a rematch later in the week.

Becky called, "Mommy, Mr Dimmie, come see! Three birds sharing a log." The adults moved to the rail. For a moment, Dimmie wondered what it would be like to have a family of his own. A cute little daughter to play with, a pretty wife to talk to, a home of his own without Mam and Gran telling him what to do all the time.

No, that wasn't in the cards for him.

But why not? Who did Lucky think he was, telling his boys how to live their lives?

The captain's voice came over the PA system. "Howdy, *Ocean Serenity*! Time for your noon report, but first, your daily joke. What lays on the bottom of the ocean and twitches?"

"Shh-hh, I want to hear this." A man elbowed his wife. "What do you think it is?"

"Some kind of a crab, most likely."

"A *nervous wreck*." The captain chuckled. "Look, folks, I don't write it, I only read it. Our current location is—"

Chapter twenty-two

Dimmie glanced at his wristwatch, a gift from Mam and Gran when he finished his probation program last year. Noon already? Where had the morning gone? He wanted to find old man Kerrick today, so he could keep an eye on him on the bus tour in Bar Harbor tomorrow. Brody said Eye Tee Guy had reserved a spot for him; the ticket was in the folder. He'd wasted too much time walking the ship, and getting himself out of that comfortable bed, too.

Becky pulled at Jill's hand. "Mommy, Mommy, can we go in the pool now? Mr Dimmie, will you come swimming with us?"

Dimmie blinked. He hesitated, unsure if Brody packed swimming trunks for him. His old green plaid ones were home in his top bureau drawer. "I'll come sit by you, if that's okay with your mother, then I gotta find some food. My stomach's growling like a bear."

Laughing, Jill and Becky linked arms and headed for the curling staircase. "Sure, come along, we'll order something from the grill on the pool deck."

Ten minutes later, they'd staked out three lounge chairs, ordered burgers, and Becky was already in the pool. Dimmie relaxed, arranging a cushion behind his head. "This is the life!"

"Isn't it wonderful?" Jill giggled, her eyes sparkling. "Dimmie, can I tell you a secret? I don't want

Becky to know, but I'm going to burst if I don't tell *somebody*."

Dimmie sat up straight. "Me? You want to tell me a secret? Sure, I'm all ears for you."

"You see, it's my husband. Becky told you he's serving in the Middle East. I got word last week, before we left home, that he was granted a leave. Only four days, before his unit moves closer to the front. I told him we'd skip this cruise, fly anywhere to meet him, but he said, no, he'd meet us in Portland. I haven't seen him in so long—!"

"Closer to the front?"

"I'm not going to let myself think about that. But I get to see him!"

"Good for you, Jill." Dimmie swallowed an unfamiliar emotion. Envy? No, this was raw jealousy, strong enough to curdle a man's soul. Man, her husband was a lucky schmuck.

"Mommy, watch me jump, Mommy! Mr Dimmie, look at me!" Even from a distance, Becky's energy was contagious.

"Good one, Becky! Now, come dry off, your lunch is almost ready. You can get back in after you eat." Jill held up a striped towel. "Dimmie, please don't tell Becky about her dad. The military changes its mind so often; I don't want to get her hopes up. In case something happens, you know."

"You got it." Dimmie forced a smile. "He'll be so happy to see you both."

"I know, and I can't wait! You're a good friend."

Becky kept up a happy chatter as they polished off burgers and fries, covering the fact that Dimmie had nothing to say. How could he sit with another man's family like he had a right to be there? As soon as the waiter removed the last greasy paper napkin, he stood. "Thanks, ladies. I have to…to…check on something. See you around."

Jill threw him a jaunty wink and Becky headed back to the pool. Some guys had all the luck.

Earlier, he'd passed a sports bar on deck ten. Old men liked bars, right? It was as good a place as any to look for the old mob boss. Plenty of time. He still thought a cruise ship was the wrong place for a hit; all these happy people on vacation. On the other hand, any place outside of the city was the wrong place, in his mind. And so long as he was careful, none of the vacationers would even suspect. He knew how to do his job. Like Gran always said, this wasn't his first radio. He wasn't sure what radios had to do with skill, but Gran said that a lot.

The sports bar reminded him of O'Malley's in the city. Some soccer game playing on the big screen, same dim lighting, same round tables, the same feeling of comradery he'd seen watching Lucky Callahan laughing with his cronies. Dimmie took a seat at the end of the shiny bar and waved his card at the bartender. He'd planned on ordering a root beer, but the bartender nodded and slid a foamy mug of beer down the length of the bar. Dimmie grabbed it before it hit the bronze lip. Who was to know?

He grinned as a waiter placed a grilled hot dog and chips in front of him. What a deal; he hadn't even ordered. "You got any french fries?" he ventured. Soon after, the waiter slid a plate of fries and some fried oval things in front of him. Dimmie gingerly bit through the batter. A spicy pepper filled with molten white cheese exploded in his mouth. He'd never tasted anything like it before. He waved the waiter over. "Bring me another foot long, and more of these...What do you call 'em?"

"Jalapeno poppers, sir."

"Holly-what? More, when you get a chance." Dimmie sipped his beer, at last remembering to look for the old mob boss. No, only young guys here. May as well watch the game. Kerrick wasn't going anywhere.

"Yo, man, what's the score?"

Chapter twenty-three

Although Dimmie ate a burger and two plates of fries by the pool and two hot dogs, more fries, and a heap of jalapeno poppers in the bar, he decided to brave the main dining room for dinner a few hours later. The grilled hot dogs in the bar were like nothing he'd ever tasted, browned and crusty on poppy seed buns, not like the boiled ones on the street corners in the city. He made up his mind to try something new for dinner, too. Maybe he'd like it just as well. These cruise cooks knew what they were doing.

Seated at his designated table with nine other passengers, Dimmie stared at the menu. He recognized lasagna, and a T-bone was meat. He knew that, but some of the other items baffled him. A tomato and buffalo mozzarella salad? Buffaloes were like huge cows, he'd seen them on TV, but who'd ever milk one to make cheese? What was salmon tartare? Duck confit sounded like something to avoid. Was it made of ducks like the ones on the ponds in Central Park, the ones that pooped green slime every few feet?

Engrossed in the menu, Dimmie didn't notice the waiter approach his chair. On the second, "Sir, for you?" he looked up. He hadn't decided what to order, but with all eyes on him, he had to make up his mind and quick. Mute, he pointed at several items on the menu.

"Very good, Sir," the waiter nodded. "Escargot, hen-of-the-woods consommé, veal Marsala with peach aspic on the side, and for dessert?"

Remembering Becky's burger the first day, Dimmie
ventured, "You got anything besides what's on the menu?
Ice cream, maybe?"

"Yes, sir, of course. After a heavy meal, I
recommend the lime sorbet." The waiter moved to the
passenger on Dimmie's left.

Wondering what a sore-bay was, Dimmie sat back
and took in his tablemates. The three women with German
accents were mother and two sisters; he'd overheard them
talking as they took their seats. Next to him was a young
couple who couldn't keep their hands to themselves. Good
thing Mam wasn't here or she'd have put them in their
place with one raised eyebrow. A slap if they didn't shape
up. A middle-aged couple sat across from Dimmie. They
gazed around the three-tiered dining room, pointing out
paintings and sculptures to each other. They didn't look
like art thieves to Dimmie. Perhaps they just liked the style.

To his right was a woman in her mid-70s or so; it
was hard to tell under all that make up. She kept patting the
man next to her with a wrinkled hand, with at least two
rings on every finger. No, not her left ring finger; Dimmie
heard her cackling to the man next to her about how she'd
come on the ship with the sole intent of filling that finger.

"So many lovely older gentlemen onboard, but
none as handsome as you. Traveling alone, are you?"

The old man recoiled, sinking into his chair as far
out of her reach as he could manage, looking like he'd
rather be just about anywhere else. He reached for the

bread basket, only to have the loud woman grab the roll from his hand. "Let me butter that for you, darlin', I just love doing for a good-looking man. Did you hear there's a dance club onboard?"

"You like escargot, do you?" The woman across the table smiled at Dimmie. "Pretty brave, I'd say, to eat snails. Not for me. I hear the garlic butter is the best part, but I say, why not eat the garlic butter and skip the escargot?"

Dimmie sat back, wondering what on earth she was talking about. Nobody said anything about snails, and Mam would say that wasn't decent dinnertime conversation. What was ess cargo? Mam taught him to speak when spoken to, that was manners, so he said, "I like garlic and butter. On 42nd Avenue, there's an Italian joint with the best garlic bread in the world." He noticed the old man shoot him a glance. "Dripping with butter and plenty of garlic. My mother always says I gotta eat mints the next day after eating that, but what are you gonna do?"

The woman laughed. "You're from New York City, aren't you? Larry and I are from Minneapolis, but I'd recognize your accent anywhere. You sound just like a character from the old gangster movies." She sipped her water.

Red-faced, Dimmie mumbled, "I don't have any accent!"

Conversation swirled, but Dimmie didn't have much to contribute. As the tablemates introduced themselves, he noticed the old man at the end eying him.

Something familiar about him. Ah, well, old guys were all alike.

"What do you do for a living?" was a standard question. Dimmie knew better than to answer that. "Is this your first cruise?" turned the conversation to better place. Once he admitted it was, advice flew from every quarter. The main gist was that he had to read, read, read, so as not to miss anything. Dimmie wasn't much for reading, and his name wasn't Jimmy, either. He'd said that twice, but no one heard him.

Before long, the waiter was back with a tray of appetizers. Dimmie breathed in the steam from a round raised dish in front of him. Melted white cheese swam on top, inviting him to dip a crusty breadstick into the sauce. He glanced at the others at the table, who were turning their attention to soup and salad. Dimmie dug in with the tiny toy fork on the plate. He pulled up something round and popped it in his mouth.

He gagged and cast his eyes around frantically, seeing no way to spit it out and still use his manners. There was no way he was going to swallow that chewy, gritty thing.

The older man two chairs down smiled. While the woman between them squeezed a lime wedge on her salad, he leaned behind her and advised Dimmie, "Spit it out onto your spoon and set it on the plate, young man. You don't have to eat it; your mother will never know. Escargot reminds me of pencil erasers, aye."

With a grateful nod, Dimmie spit the offending morsel onto the plate and concentrated on the garlic butter and soft breadsticks. The old man gave good advice, but how did he know about Mam's rule of finishing everything on his plate? Maybe he had a mother of his own. The man sounded like he was from the City, a kindred spirit among strangers. Dimmie turned to speak to him, but the large woman blocked his way, gales of laughter ensuing as she told a story about her "dear *late* husband, who wanted me to be happy. I'm sure *you* could make me happy, couldn't you?"

Dimmie felt sorry for the old guy. A man should be able to eat in peace. He moved the escargot around on the dish so the waiter wouldn't think he didn't like it. That was manners, too. The cook might be insulted if it looked untouched, and Dimmie knew better than to anger a cook.

He reconsidered when the waiter replaced the escargot with consommé. It looked like watery apple juice, tasted like dirty fingernails, and they must have forgotten to put the noodles and vegetables in it. What kind of a cook was in the kitchen, anyway? Listening to the conversation swirl around him, Dimmie made the best of his meal. If he was still hungry, he could stop by the buffet later. At least there, he could see what he was getting. Maybe there'd be some pavlova, leftover from lunch.

Chapter twenty-four

Before he went to his cabin for bed, Dimmie stood by the rail on the upper deck. This far from shore, the only lights beyond the ship's lights were stars. The black water swirled far below him. He'd had no idea there was this much water on all the earth, much less all in one place. The openness made his stomach feel funny, but he was not as dizzy if he kept one hand on the railing.

Maybe it was dinner churning his guts. He was still upset about the escargot. It wasn't honest to make it sound like a fancy dish when it was really just cooked garden snails with garlic butter. Like the zucchini bread Mrs Tom brought over last summer. It looked like dessert, but the green flecks didn't hide the fact she'd hidden vegetables in it. It wasn't honest at all. He'd be more careful tomorrow.

He'd scanned the dining room over dinner, trying to spot Kerrick. The woman across the table said to her companion what a nervous young man he was. Dimmie heard the guy reply something about first time cruisers and how excitable they can be. Realizing they were talking about him, Dimmie turned his focus to his dinner. *Me, excitable? Never.* Gingerly taking bites of what turned out to be just beef with a red sauce, he'd still kept an eye out for Kerrick in the dining room. The old boss had to eat sometime.

He ran his hand over the cool railing. A man could get hurt and hurt bad if he fell overboard. No, the railing was higher than his waist; an accident would be unlikely.

Dimmie thought about the old men he'd known. He was pretty sure he could throw any of them overboard, especially if he had the upper hand or the element of surprise. That was Lucky's phrase; he was always telling Dimmie to get the element of surprise when he ordered a hit, as if Dimmie didn't know how to do his job.

He'd killed a lot more men than Lucky, but Lucky was one to tell people what they already knew, making himself out to be the expert. Full of himself, Mam would say, if she knew him better. For all Mam knew, Lucky was just some guy she passed on the street by the market sometimes. She'd kill him herself if she knew he'd recruited Dimmie.

During the muster drill (Dimmie didn't know why they called it that; he didn't hear anything about mustard, or see any, either), the voice on the loud speaker said if anybody saw anybody fall overboard, they were supposed to holler, "Man Overboard" right away, and throw something down in the water, something that would float. That made sense if you wanted to save somebody. But if he could find Colin Kerrick, throw him over the rail with nobody looking, and wait a few minutes before yelling "Man Overboard", chances are, it'd be too late to save him.

Dimmie was meticulous about not making messes when he worked. He hated to leave a lot of blood for somebody to clean up. A body in the big wide ocean would be perfect. Nobody would ever find the old man. He patted the railing, his mind made up. Maybe tomorrow night, after the bus tour in Bar Harbor; he'd identify his mark on the tour and get it done. He could do this job, even without his Rugar or favorite knife. Now, he just had to *find* Kerrick.

And the ice cream shop on the pool deck, too. Imagine, all the ice cream he could eat, free for the asking, and no Mam here to remind him about avoiding sweets! When else could he eat ice cream right before bed? His cabin would wait.

This is the life.

Chapter twenty-five

Bar Harbor, Maine

Dimmie hadn't worn a sticker on his shirt since he was in the kindergarten class at Saint Margaret's. He suppressed the urge to pick off the yellow Group Three oval, but the crew lady who placed it there said he had to wear it all day so they'd know who belonged on which tour bus. Dimmie wondered for the thousandth time who this "they" was.

Before the group even boarded the big blue bus, Dimmie had his eye on the man in the blue shirt, the one with the fat wife by his side. Lucky hadn't mentioned Kerrick having a wife with him, but that didn't mean anything. She was probably shopping when Lucky saw Kerrick in the subway. Or maybe Lucky didn't notice her. He made a big deal about everything, but Dimmie knew a lot got by him, not like the old boss.

The old man's name was Darren; he knew that because he overheard him introduce himself to the man behind him. "I don't like strangers. I'm better off meeting everybody, so there's no strangers near me." He reached his hand across the aisle next. "Good day to you. This is my wife, Ginny. My name is Darren, Darren Crandall."

Sure, it was. Darren's Irish accent seemed faded, but Dimmie felt a chill like when the boys stuffed the back of his shirt with snow. His ear caught the lilt; he'd heard it all his life. He looked closer, keeping his face behind the seat back so Colin Kerrick—if that's who he was, and it had to be—wouldn't see him.

The age was right. Darren had a louder voice than Dimmie recalled, and the boss in his memory wasn't such a glad-hander, but so many years had passed. He was just a kid when Kerrick did what he did. He made up his mind to keep an eye on the older man for the rest of the day. After all, Brody said the Eye Tee guy had confirmed Colin Kerrick was on the bus tour. This had to be him.

Dimmie kept his eyes out the window as the bus rolled though the green countryside. Now that he knew right where Kerrick was, he could relax. So much forest and rolling farmland, dotted with little ponds here and there. Like Central Park, only it went on for miles. The nuns in school said the middle part of American had a lot of open land, but he hadn't known it was true just a couple of days from New York City, too.

At one point, the driver pulled over to the shoulder to show off a beaver dam in a small lake. The passengers oohed and ahhed, as excited as if they'd constructed it themselves. His uneasiness about leaving the city was fading. Sure, everything was unfamiliar, but maybe that billboard he'd seen at the port was right. *Different doesn't mean bad.*

He strained to listen to Darren amid the swirling conversations on the bus. The old guy talked about the city like he owned the place, the best bodegas, where to get the best cheesecake in town, said he felt most alive at night when the city lights came on and the sunlight faded. Dimmie nodded; he felt like that, too. Once the tourists headed for their rented beds, the real work of the city got underway.

"The wife here, she likes to travel," Darren said, "but me? If I never had to leave the 202 again, I'd die a happy man. Give me a slice and a black and white. That's all I ask."

His wife chimed in, "And your fedora. You're the only man I know who still wears a hat in public."

He guffawed, doffing his hat. "A fedora and a trench coat never go out of style in my book. Why, in my old line of work, me and the boys never…"

Dimmie sat back, his face warming. He wished he could hear better. How could the old boss talk so openly about the mob like that?

Just then, the young woman behind him let out a shrieking laugh, drowning out the old mob boss' words.

"I'm Joni and this is my *husband,* Tony, Cute, huh? I just love saying *husband.* We're on our *honeymoon.*"

A blonde across the aisle squealed, "Ooh, how exciting! Tell me all about your wedding, every little detail. Was it the best day ever?"

As the story unfolded, Dimmie longed to change seats to get away from the woman's high-pitched voice, closer to the old man. He scanned the bus; the only empty seats were way in the back.

"Oh, it was the *sweetest* thing in the history of *ever*! We invited our friends, Kim and Casey, to go on this *cruise* with us. We didn't tell them it was for our *honeymoon*. Kim, Casey! Say *hi* to the nice folks. *Anyway*, we had the driver stop at a *park* on the way to the pier and there was our minister, *right* where we told him to be. And my *sister*, with a *big* bouquet of daisies, my *very* favorite flower on *earth.*"

"Wait—what? A minister and flowers?" The young woman squealed. "In a park? You did *not!*"

"Oh, yes, we *did*. Kim and Casey were our witnesses, and as *soon* as the minister signed the marriage certificate, we *raced* for the ship. What could be better than a honeymoon with our *very best* friends in the *whole* wide world?"

Congratulations came from all directions. Dimmie noticed the old mob boss was silent, for once, looking out the window. His wife tugged at the front of her blue blouse, her eyes down. Maybe the boss's marriage wasn't as happy as the young couple's. What did Gran always say?

"Nothing is as it seems."

Chapter twenty-six

Colin stared out the window, unseeing, lost in his own thoughts. What was he doing trapped on a bus? On the one hand, it was good to be with people who had no idea who he was. On the other hand, a guided tour of Acadia Park wasn't what he felt like doing today, even though the green scenery was a nice change from Nebraska's endless prairie. It had sounded like a good idea when the travel agent threw in the tour for free, but he should have stayed on the ship. Maybe showing his face in public was a bad idea. Wasn't that what the witness protection program was designed for, to keep him hidden?

And that young fellow, the one with the shock of red hair…what was he doing on a cruise ship? He had recognized him right away, but the younger man hadn't given him a second glance, focused instead on the man with the plump wife toward the front of the bus. The man was so loud, it was hard to ignore him. His poor wife. But at least they were together. Seeing other married couples made him miss Ellie even more.

Decades ago, he fell in love with the most beautiful girl in high school, and the smartest, too. She had a way of drawing people to her, and he was determined to be the closest of all. He skillfully nudged any potential suitors out of the picture. Before long, she had eyes for only him. After senior year, they married. She always said, "High school sweethearts, and sweethearts forever," like one of those bumper stickers. Colin was a lucky man and he knew it.

The two poor Irish kids had no money to speak of. He did very well for himself in the business, but that came years later. Still, his beloved dreamed of a luxurious honeymoon. "Maybe even Niagara Falls, like the swells, or I guess the Jersey shore will do." The Jersey shore was no great shakes; anybody could go there. He called in some markers and pocketed enough for a passenger train to Buffalo the day after their wedding. Anything to make his bride smile. He'd figure out a hotel once they arrived.

They held hands on the train, watching the scenery rush by. Leaving New York city was a rare event; neither had been this far west, and she exclaimed over the passing farms and cows. At one train station, they had a two-hour layover and spent it walking near the new Erie Canal. She joked, saying he should go to college and become an engineer, as intent as he was on watching the process, but they both knew his path was already set in stone. They sipped lemonade from a tiny tea shop before they reboarded the train.

At last, she dozed on his shoulder and he smiled, happier than he could have imagined. He surveyed their future. Up and coming, he had to keep his fingers on a hundred threads or the whole thing might come unraveled. Even a week away left him vulnerable, but how often did a man get a honeymoon vacation with a beautiful woman?

A couple of other passengers motioned for him to join them in the salon car. He gently nudged his bride's head onto a cushion and followed the men. Minutes later, deep in a poker game and three hands ahead, he got to talking to a priest. Fresh off the boat from Italy, the prelate was on his way to a rectory near Niagara Falls, and not a bad player, considering his background and all.

Congratulating him on his marriage, the priest offered a place to stay in the rectory. "It won't be fancy, but it'll save you some money. I need to make a good first impression on the Father, and what's better than serving others?"

Dubious at first, the young man accepted the offer. For years afterwards, Ellie told about falling asleep in each other's arms to the sound of Gregorian chants from the chapel below. She always said it was the funniest honeymoon she'd ever heard of, her blue eyes sparkling. He knew the priest must have taken some flak for showing up with newlyweds in tow. The Irish and Italians were not on good terms back then. Relations hadn't improved much. Yet there were good people all around, and that kindness helped the newlyweds get off to a good start.

A shout of laughter brought him back to the present. The bus was stopping at a pullout, and the guide said something about walking down to a blowhole on the rocks down the path. Blowholes, he didn't know, but he recognized a blow hard when he heard one. Who'd ever take friends on a honeymoon? And he hadn't heard what became of the bride's sister. Left on the pier likely, still holding the daisies.

Chapter twenty-seven

Imagine having enough money to throw around, like the Carnegies and Rockefellers had back in the day? It was more than Dimmie could take in. Acadia Park probably cost more than the take he saw on Lucky's desk last year, all those duffle bags of cash, zipped open. Dimmie wasn't supposed to see it. "Stay in the hall," Lucky had ordered, but he couldn't resist one peek.

Julie, the guide, explained the trails through Acadia Park were formerly carriage trails for the rich people who lived here long ago, and they donated the land, making sure it stayed a park forever. Like Central Park, where even the skyscrapers had to respect its boundaries.

So much quiet! Birds, water lapping at the shore, some scurrying creature chirruped by that log; no familiar traffic or cars honking or people shouting like in the city. Even the passengers, who had talked up a storm on the bus, lowered their voices, or maybe the trees muffled the sound.

He breathed in the chilly air, pausing on one of the stone bridges arching over a wide gravel horse trail while most of the group meandered on ahead. If he could find a way to get Kerrick alone, a simple shove over the railing would do it, and look like an accident, too. Not being seen would be the problem. His wife clung to him like she was afraid something bad would happen to him if she left him alone. Well, she was right.

The guide brought up the rear, slowing beside Dimmie. "You about ready for lunch, Sir?" Julie smiled, her copper hair shining in the light. "Next stop is the lobster pound, with wild blueberry pie for dessert."

Dimmie stepped back. "Lobster pound? You mean like them dog pounds they have in the city?"

"*Dog* pound? That's a good one!" She laughed, her too-white teeth glinting. "I'll remember that one. We'd better head back to the bus." Raising her voice, she called, "Walk this way, people, we're walking, we're walking. Next on the agenda: lunch on a bay so pretty, you'll think you fell into a postcard."

The passengers chatted as they lined up to board the bus. A man next to Dimmie elbowed him on the bus steps. "Man, a fresh lobster pulled out of the ocean this morning! I can't think of a better meal, can you?"

Dimmie tried to smile back. He admitted he didn't think he could eat a lobster, not after the escargot last night. Lobsters look like big red roaches to him. Maybe they'd have a boiled potato or something he could stomach.

The man raised an eyebrow as he slipped into his seat. "What are you doing on this tour, man, if you're not here for the lobster?"

Before long, the bus pulled up to a storm-blown shack on the shore of a calm bay, surrounded by red picnic tables. The passengers wandered down the dock to take pictures of the lobster pots, then took their places at the tables. Dimmie managed to be seated at the far end of the table where Kerrick and his wife sat, along with five others.

The old guy was chattering on about tonight's show back on the ship. "Love those shows; never miss a one. Not as good as Broadway—" He sure became a chatterbox once he entered the witness protection program! Maybe he'd been keeping it all inside all those years. Some people were like that. Mam said the man on the fourth floor never said a word until his brother moved in with him, then he talked like he'd been keeping all of those words behind a dam that burst when Tom walked in. Couldn't hardly shut the man up now.

They donned plastic lobster bibs amid much laughter. Dimmie left his bib folded by his fork. He wasn't a baby. His stomach churned; whether from hunger or trepidation about a lobster, he didn't know. Staring at the gentle waves seemed to help. He should have eaten a bigger breakfast. Those powdered-sugar donuts were sure good.

Julie clapped her hands. "Lunch will be out in a moment. First, I have a joke. Ready? Why don't lobsters share?" She paused. "Give up? Because they're *shell*fish, get it?" She waved her hand over the chuckles and boos. "Here come the lobsters. Enjoy, folks!"

White-aproned servers placed big bowls of boiled red potatoes and corn on the cob on the tables, followed by a two-pound lobster and a cup of drawn butter at each person's place. Dimmie's stomach protested. How could he avoid the shiny red creatures without getting heckled? It wasn't the kind of food he could just push around with a fork. The lobsters' legs reminded him of spiders, dead ones, the ones he found in the windowsills with their legs fold up.

"There you are, I was looking for you. I heard you say you're not a lobster fan, so I picked this up while they were cooking." The bus driver set a paper bag in front of Dimmie with a smile. "I didn't know if you liked fries or rings, so I got you both."

Dimmie dumped out a loaded double cheeseburger, onion rings, a bag of french fries, and four ketchup packets. He grinned at the driver. "You did this for me? Man, you just earned your tip."

The driver laughed and walked toward the lobster shack. "Hey, Mack, you got a lobster roll for me?"

Dimmie sunk his teeth into the thick burger, holding it with both hands. All around him, people ripped into the fresh lobsters, smacking their lips, cracking shells, sucking the juice from the legs. Dimmie tried to block out the sounds.

"Pass down the paper towels, will you?"

Dimmie reached for the roll in the middle of the table and handed it to the man on his left, the one who'd been eyeing him all morning. What was with the man, anyway? Maybe Dimmie reminded him of a grandson or somebody. Old guys were like that.

"What, you're not even going to try the lobster? Son, you're missing out, aye. You gotta at least try a bite. For the Old Country." The man extended a fork with a quivering chunk of lobster meat on it. "Come on, young fella, give it a taste."

One bite, for the Old Country. Dimmie frowned, wishing the man would leave him alone; he'd been too close all morning. He swallowed the lobster meat whole so no morsel could stick in his teeth, then chucked an onion ring in after it. Back to the burger.

Julie walked to the table. "Do I hear a lilt of Irish? Where are you all from, may I ask?"

Dutifully, each person at the table responded. Toronto, Baltimore, Albany. The man at the far end of the picnic table deflected quickly, before his wife could respond. "We've been around. Where is anybody from, really?"

Julie chuckled. "You have a point, Sir." She moved to the next table.

Dimmie smiled to himself; yup, that was old man Kerrick, all right. Everybody else knew where they were from. Once a man went into witness protection, maybe he lost his sense of home. He popped the last three french fries into his mouth and stuffed the wrappers into the bag. While the others finished eating, he wandered down to the dock, away from the endless crunching of lobster shells.

He'd keep an eye on the group. Mam said his sweet tooth was bigger than his head. He didn't understand how that could be, but he wasn't going to miss the wild blueberry pie.

Half an hour later, they boarded the bus. As it rolled out, someone called, "Hey, wait, stop, we're missing somebody. Remember the loud guy with the blue shirt?"

"He said his wife wasn't feeling well, so they took a cab back to the ship." Julie said, "We'll be passing Somes Sound, the only fjord on the east coast of North America, in a few minutes, so be on the lookout for…"

Dimmie relaxed for the first time in days. Kerrick must have felt Dimmie watching him throughout the morning; why else would be have left the group so suddenly? He'd watch for his opportunity to take out the old boss back on the ship. For now, he might as well enjoy the tour.

He picked his teeth. The bite of lobster wasn't as bad as he expected, but that was a fine burger, even better than Billy's joint on 51st in the city.

Chapter twenty-eight

Dimmie opted for the buffet for dinner. Those little signs on each platter and bowl were reassuring; he wasn't going to fall for a trick like the escargot again. What had that old guy said? *Pencil erasers with garlic butter*, that was it. No, he'd stick to what he knew. Mam always said a man couldn't work on an empty stomach. She also said he had to eat because he was a growing boy, even though he was a man now, not a school boy. He wasn't sure if he'd find the opportunity to take out the old mobster tonight, but why take a chance?

The boss was right. There hadn't been an opportunity to kill Kerrick in Bar Harbor. The next choice was to off the old man once everybody got back on the ship. Do the job, lay low, and when the ship docked in Portland, Maine, the next morning, he was to get off the ship like he had a right to be there. No problem. He just needed a plan.

After he added a thick prime rib to his plate, he headed for a table by the window. The waiter brought him a glass of lemonade and a steak knife. "You might need this. Can I get anything else for you?"

Dimmie stammered his thanks, staring at the knife. How often did anybody put a weapon right in his hands? It must have been a sign from heaven, as Gran often said. Maybe leaving his blade at home was all right after all. Chewing his potatoes, Dimmie debated. He hadn't found where the old mobster's cabin was located — he'd planned to follow him after the tour— but he knew he and his wife would be at the show tomorrow night. He'd trail him then. If he was extra lucky, maybe the old guy would step away from his clingy wife for a few minutes. Maybe she really wasn't feeling well, as they said at lunch. In that case, he'd have a clear shot.

After dinner, he'd wipe the steak knife clean, wrap it in one of those fancy napkins and stick it in his pocket. Lucky always said he had to make his priorities, and that chocolate cake over there was the biggest Dimmie had ever seen. First, the prime rib.

Seeing he had twenty minutes before the show started, Dimmie ducked out onto the open Promenade deck for some air. Mam always said to go outside for some air. Dimmie thought air was pretty much everywhere, but he did think the air on the deck smelled good, fresher, salty. He wasn't sure what an aerialist was, but the show was free and there was nobody to tell him he couldn't go.

Maybe he'd get a glimpse of Colin Kerrick, tail him back to his cabin, find a way to finish the old guy. Once the hit was done, he could enjoy the rest of the evening, then get off the ship when it docked in Portland in the morning. Maybe he'd even sleep in, take his time getting off. When else would he ever again get a chance to set foot on a cruise ship? Breakfast this morning was a feast.

A passenger by the rail commented, "Looks like the weather's taking a turn. With this cloud bank rolling in, we'll be socked in in no time. I wonder if we'll be able to get into port tomorrow."

The ship uttered a low, prolonged groan and Dimmie jumped. "What was that?"

"What did I tell you? That's the ship's foghorn. It'll probably go on all night. Get used to it, kid."

Bar Harbor receded in the distance, its lights muffled in the fog. Dimmie brushed off the fine mist that dampened his shirt and turned back toward the theatre. He decided to sit in the balcony tonight, where he could have a good view of the performers and the audience below. He climbed the stairs and found a seat on the front row. Taking a breath, he leaned forward, his eyes taking in each row of the packed theater. He muttered, "Looks like a box of Gran's Q-tips, all those white heads in rows." Before he could locate the mob boss, the house lights dimmed.

The band started up. A single spotlight illuminated a woman seated on a hoop suspended above the stage, covered in sparkles. Dimmie squinted, trying to make out if she was wearing anything at all under all that glitter. With a coquettish smile, she spun the hoop, her blonde hair streaming behind her. Faster and faster she spun, the hoop slowly lowering until she slipped free and dropped to the stage, accepting the warm applause with a deep bow.

The music changed to a pop tune, and, as the audience clapped along, twelve costumed dancers paraded onto the stage, waving huge feathered fans. Dimmie settled back into his seat. He couldn't see Kerrick in the dark anyway; may as well take in the show. Their bright costumes reminded him of the musicals he and Gran watched at the Dollar Cinema in Hell's Kitchen once or twice a year, only these were real performers on a real stage. And Gran would have squawked at those costumes. Some of the feathers barely covered the dancers' rear ends. This was the life.

As the house lights came on at intermission, he patted the steak knife in his pocket, wrapped in a linen napkin. He felt bad for stealing it from the buffet. It wasn't really stealing, though. Borrowing, more like. He was planning on putting the knife back when he went to the buffet for breakfast.

Maybe somebody kept count of these things like they did in the juvie center. He didn't know why, but he knew keeping track of knives and forks was a big deal in juvie. It might be a big deal on cruise ships, too; maybe even more so, he didn't know. He didn't want anybody to get in trouble if the knife count came up short.

He had a job to do and Lucky said to do it. In the bright house lights, he scanned the rows below him on the main floor. His heart leaped; that was definitely the old man from the tour bus. Colin Kerrick and his wife sat in the second row from the back, middle section, both wearing navy blue. Their row was full, but as Dimmie watched, four people in the row behind the old mob boss walked out. He took a deep breath.

Sean would call it an opportunity, having a space open up like that. Gran would call it the hand of God, but Dimmie was pretty sure the Good Lord Above wasn't about to help him murder a man. The Bible had some stuff to say about killing. The Bible was written by old men along ago; they had no idea what it was like to work for Lucky Callahan.

All he had to do was move to that row, do the job, and he'd have a clear path to slip into the corridor. But when? How could he cover himself? Sometimes when Dimmie did a hit, the victim made noise or tried to struggle. This time, he had to prevent that. It had to be a clean hit with nobody the wiser.

There was no room to run on a cruise ship.

Chapter twenty-nine

Dimmie's answer came as the house lights dimmed for the second act. Applause rocked the theatre, taking on a life of its own, as three performers swung on trapeze bars above the audience, its energy nearly drowning out the ship's foghorn. Dimmie noticed the foghorn sounded every ninety-five seconds. He could count on the sound to help cover him and if people kept clapping, that'd help, too.

How did that girl stay on the skinny bar without falling off?

He made his way down the spiral staircase to the lower level and slipped into the empty seat behind the old man. No reason to miss the rest of the show. When would he have another chance to sit in a glitzy theatre? Enthralled by the trapeze artist, Dimmie nevertheless kept an eye on Kerrick. It was him, all right, the man from the tour; he even held a fedora on his lap. Guess his wife was feeling better, if she'd really been sick in the first place. She had sure gobbled up her lobster at lunch with a hearty appetite, and here she was, apparently healthy enough to attend the show.

The dancers swirled long streamers onstage in the final scene. *Final scene,* Dimmie thought, slowing his breathing as he'd done a hundred times or more. There was a rhythm to his work, same as a dancer's, only not the same at all. As the music softened, the performers held hands center stage and took a bow. The aerialist stepped in front, and the audience rose as one in a standing ovation. The cheering rocked the theater; he could feel it pulsing though his feet. Dimmie edged closer to his prey, yet he couldn't help admiring the performer on stage. Turned out, she was wearing a skin-colored leotard under the sparkles. Gran would still not approve, but it beat being naked in front of so many people like he thought at first. A few sparkles weren't enough to be decent.

As the audience applause increased, Dimmie slid the steak knife from his pants pocket. He unwrapped it from the linen napkin, covering the blade with his left hand against any glint of light, keeping it below the seat cushion. Out of sight, should anyone be looking.

The band picked up the pace, and the dancers went into an encore number. The audience settled back into the plush seats, clapping with the drum beat, the only lights in the theater focused on the headliners on stage. Man, that woman could sing.

Dimmie leaned over the old man. Both hands on his shoulders, he whispered, "I'm sorry, but the boss said I gotta do what I'm told to stay alive. Too bad you didn't stay gone when you went away." The old man jerked his head, but not fast enough.

With a quick motion, Dimmie reached around and jabbed the knife into the front of the man's throat, feeling the familiar resistance at first. Sean had told him if you're going to kill a man who's sitting down, that was the way to do it. You cut their breath right out of them and they can't even holler. Sean had a talent, that was for sure. Too bad he had to be in the river.

A jab, a twist, and not even his wife noticed. Dimmie wiped the blade on the old man's shoulder. He didn't want to get blood on his new pants. The stage lights came on just as Dimmie stuffed the knife back in his pocket. The job was done, and not a sound from old Kerrick. His dark blue shirt even hid the blood.

The stage lights blinked twice and dimmed again as the cruise director came from stage left. He waved his hands and the audience quieted, waiting for his usual announcements. He called for "A little more love for our production team." More applause, weaker now, a reminder about the live band playing in the lounge on deck twelve, and the audience rose, slowly filling the aisles. Somebody muttered about how long it took to get out of the theatre. The slowest passengers always clogged the exits.

Dimmie waited for an older woman to pass his row. He filed out in turn, whispering a silent prayer for the man's soul. Mam always prayed for the souls of the dead people she knew. Gran even prayed for people she read about in the newspaper. Obituaries page, that's what Mam called it. They always prayed for the souls of the dead in mass on Sunday mornings, too. To Dimmie, it sounded like a chant, like that conga line dance he saw in a movie a long time ago. Cha-chaa, go to *heaVEN*, Cha-chaa, go to *heaVEN*, over and over again in his mind.

As he moved up the aisle, into the crowded corridor, veering left toward the Promenade doors, he chanted in his mind, Kerrick, go to *heaVEN*, Kerrick, go to *heaVEN*. He wasn't sure if God actually wanted Colin

Kerrick in heaven, but he'd leave that up to Him to figure
out.

It was like Mr Andy down the hall at home said
about his time in Vietnam. He said his philosophy was
"Kill them all and let God sort them out." Dimmie didn't
know if Andy had killed them all, or killed anybody at all,
for that matter. Sometimes he wished he could talk to Mr
Andy, maybe learn some tips on killing. Maybe he was a
skilled killer when he was younger, but now, Andy was just
an old man with shaky hands who left bags of empty wine
bottles outside his apartment door. Mam said Mr Andy was
damaged. War did things to people, she said.

A scream rang out, a piercing scream, and the
crowd stopped in its tracks. Another, another…the screams
kept on coming, like a soundtrack stuck on repeat.
Passengers froze like those performers on Times Square.
Dimmie glanced back into the theatre. A cluster of
passengers tightened like a knot in a shoelace, near where
Dimmie had been sitting. The screams stopped. He could
hear a woman, high pitched and talking fast.

"My husband! Oh, *Darren*! He's bleeding! He's
dead, isn't he? Darren!" She screamed again, over and
over.

Chapter thirty

"Dead? What happened?"

Frantic voices exclaimed, "Who's dead? Is somebody hurt?"

A man pushed by Dimmie and punched numbers on the phone on the wall. "We need help. A man is injured in the theatre. Blood everywhere. I think it's his neck. I don't know. He just didn't stand up when the show ended. He— just send help, okay?"

Dimmie felt a squirming in his stomach, like a mouse climbing around in there. He didn't know if it was from nerves or maybe he just needed a snack. Sometimes when he was hungry, it felt wiggly. Mam said nobody's stomach wiggled, but Mam wasn't here. If Mam *was* here, she'd have slapped the woman, bring her to her senses; stop that carrying on, you're making a spectacle of yourself, and everybody's looking at you. Don't make such a scene, she'd say.

The crowd divided, some rushing to get away from the scene, others pushing upstream to help or to rubberneck, he didn't know. He moved with the crowd toward the elevator bank, then detoured left onto the open deck. He'd figured out yesterday the midship elevators were mobbed after a show. By walking the length of the ship outside, he could reach the far elevators and be at the buffet before the theater emptied. His cabin steward told him he could get food there any time, day or night. Maybe they'd have more of that chocolate cake.

Too bad he had to get off the ship tomorrow morning. The other passengers still had five more days of the cruise. Lucky stiffs. He stopped in the men's room. He liked to wash his hands after a hit; it helped him forget about it, as if what he did went down the drain with the last of the soap bubbles. And, besides, there was that Noro thing Brody warned him about. Brody said it could make a guy so sick, he'd wish he was dead. Better to wash his hands.

At the buffet, Dimmie filled a plate with roast beef and cheese sandwiches and picked up a bowl of baked beans. The sandwiches were too small, doll-sized. He took four and nobody even told him to pay for them. He sat in a dim corner table near floor-to-ceiling windows that reflected like mirrors. With the fog so dense, he couldn't see a thing outside past the mist swirling in the little light on the front of the ship. Every minute and a half, the foghorn groaned.

Dimmie chewed and thought about tomorrow. The job was done. He was told to off old man Kerrick and he did it. Next: leave the ship in Portland, find the Greyhound bus station, head back to familiar turf. Brody said to leave everything onboard, except his new passport. Just smile and walk off like he was spending the day in port, like any other passenger, except keep on going. Too bad; he liked the way he looked when he caught a reflection of himself wearing the new shirts Brody bought for him. Maybe he could take just one, besides the one he had on. Who would know?

He'd better make up a story about where he'd been, too. Mam would ask—she always did, if he was gone more than a few hours—and Lucky said never to tell her about the jobs he did. Dimmie could tell her the truth this time; he was on a luxury cruise ship, but he knew she wouldn't believe him. He'd get slapped across the head like she did when she thought he was fibbing. Better to make up a story she'd believe. He took another bite. Sure enough, thick slabs of chocolate cake sat under the lights across the room, waiting for him. Extra thick frosting, too, just the way he liked it. Cake was fine, but the frosting was always the best part.

Few passengers needed a snack this time of night; the buffet was nearly empty. Idly, Dimmie listened to the buzz of nearby conversations.

"Did you hear somebody fell overboard, right off the Promenade? I saw a medical team running on deck four."

"No, that wasn't it. I heard—"

"I heard a man collapsed in the theatre. Must have been a heart attack or a stroke."

"I agree, there are a lot of old people on this ship. I've never seen so many oxygen tanks and scooters."

"*I* heard somebody fell and cut themselves. Blood everywhere."

Dimmie squirmed in his chair. The blood was always the worst part. Maybe people were under pressure, like a soda pop bottle. When a person cut themselves, blood spurted everywhere, and a neck was the worst place to cut. At least this time, in the dark theatre, he didn't have to look at it. The running-mouse feeling in his gut returned, the weight of the steak knife pressing against his leg. He forced his attention back to the baked beans. Two more bites, then the cake.

Two loud chimes rang through the buffet, and people stopped with forks midway to their mouths. An announcement, this late at night?

"Attention, if you please. You may have noticed the fog is increasing. I regret to tell you we will be unable to stop at Portland, Maine, as scheduled tomorrow. As a precaution, the port is closed to all marine traffic. I tell you this now so you will not set your wake-up calls for the morning. Our first priority is your safety. I am hopeful we'll have no trouble making our next port in Halifax, Nova Scotia." The captain's voice deepened. "On another matter, there has been a…an *incident* onboard. I expect state police to come aboard tomorrow afternoon to commence an investigation. I have every expectation you all will cooperate with them. We will have more information for you in the morning. Good evening."

Murmurs swirled through the buffet. Dimmie's stomach contracted like that time Brody punched him the stomach just to watch his face turn purple. He pushed his plate away. Too bad about the cake; no room for even the gooey frosting now.

Chapter thirty-one

Dimmie shivered in the still air. How could he ever get warm again, when his blood ran as cold as the ice water in his glass? The mobster's wife's screams echoed in his mind like a siren. So long as he concentrated on something, he could forget about it, but the minute his mind stilled, he heard her wailing all over again.

"My Darren! He's *dead*!"

Dimmie had killed a lot of men. He didn't know how many, exactly. He didn't keep a scorecard in his wallet like Sean used to, but it was more than he could count on his fingers and toes and somebody else's fingers and toes, too. Many more. Never had he heard a family member scream like that. In every case, he did the job, as Lucky ordered, and walked away, never thinking about whether the target had a family or wife or a life with people to love him in it. Had his other vics had families, too? The mice in his stomach picked up speed.

He washed his hands after every hit; how he wished he could wash that keening wail out of his ears! Why did she keep calling old Kerrick *Darren*? Maybe witness protection gave him a new identity along with a new location. That must be it.

Mam's sharp voice rammed into his thoughts. "When you see a problem, dimwit, stop and think about the best way through it. Don't go off half-cocked. You're not the sharpest tool in the shed, you know."

Dimmie didn't understand what that meant; nobody in the city had a shed, but "stop and think" sounded like what he needed to do. He sipped his water and thought hard. A plan. He needed a plan.

Lucky Callahan said to snuff out Colin Kerrick and then get off the ship in Portland, Maine. He did his part, but the captain just said the boat—no, *ship*—couldn't stop at Portland because the fog was too thick. Maybe the Good Lord Above sent the fog to cover his crime, block his getaway. Maybe the angels in heaven were mad at him for sending Kerrick there before he was ready to go.

"All done, Sir?" The waiter took the empty plates. "Can I bring you something else? Some dessert, perhaps?"

Dimmie stammered, "No, I had enough." He shuddered, the sandwiches sitting like a manhole cover in his middle. "Can I ask you a question? They said tomorrow's port is canceled. What do I do?"

The waiter explained passengers had no responsibility at all; it was like any other sea day and the cruise director's staff would most likely add other things to do activities during the day. He shifted the bar cloth in his hands. "Sir, we'll be closing this section for cleaning soon. May I—"

Dimmie took the hint and stood.

As he walked through the buffet, he slid the steak knife from his pocket and dropped it in a bin of dirty dishes. One more knife would surely go unnoticed. He walked up two decks to the open upper deck. The damp fog swirled, making wispy patterns in the ship's lights. The jogging track was deserted; most passengers chose the steamy ship's venues over the cold night air. He zipped his jacket against the chill and followed the red vinyl track, his mind churning.

Think, I have to think. Lucky said not to do any thinking, but Lucky wasn't here and neither was anybody else to tell him what to do. The good thing about the mob was that they stuck together. Here he was alone, on a cruise ship on the ocean, and nobody to knock him into line or tell him where to go next.

The boss said not to change the plan, no matter what. But the captain changed it, and Dimmie was pretty sure he hadn't talked to Lucky first. Captain said they'd have to stay on the ship tomorrow, then the next day, they'd go to Halifax, Nova Scotia. He didn't know what Nova Scotia was, but it didn't sound like the good old US of A, and he sure didn't want to end up in Halifax, not with that threat hanging over him. Halifax was in Canada and he knew Canada was a foreign country and he knew he didn't know his way around the place.

Even if he found a bus station, how would he know which one to take to the city? Did Greyhound even go to a foreign country? He didn't dare call the boss or ask questions.

Why had he let them talk him into leaving the borough? This very minute, the boys were home, safe, working for Lucky, probably laughing like they did. They'd be sleeping in their own beds tonight, too, not trapped on a fancy cruise ship with a bunch of strangers and nowhere to run to. Alone.

The boss said he was to kill Colin and make sure he was good and dead. Just do the hit, get Kerrick off his back once and for all, that's what Lucky said. Leave the ship in Portland, take the Greyhound #3521 back to the city. And "don't do any thinking." Dimmie punched a wall, glaring at a woman's raised eyebrows. She hurried through a door, seeking the nice warm corridor, not looking back.

The fog pressed against the ship like a living thing. Dimmie didn't like weather. He didn't mind daytime and he liked nighttime all right, but rain and sunshine and snow he could do without. Cold days when Mam hollered after him to wear a jacket, summer days when the heat rippled off the pavement and the NYFD opened the hydrants, rain that dripped down his neck, trudging through snow, and the wind that blew between the skyscrapers' canyons, and now this thick fog…he didn't like any of it.

And the swirling fog had changed everything, not caring one bit what he had to do. He walked on, his feet leaving wet prints on the jogging track. What was he going to do? Thoughts swirled like the lights at Rockefeller Center at Christmas time, spiraling up and up, but going nowhere.

He couldn't obey what the little boss ordered. Lucky said he had to get off in Portland, but the captain said nobody was going to get off there. The problem, as he saw it, was the captain, that bodyless voice on the loudspeaker. Maybe if he told him a story, made up a real good reason why he had to get off in Portland, the captain would let him off. Not everybody; just him.

He didn't know how to get in touch with the captain. He pulled his collar up and thought hard. He'd seen a couple of crewmembers in white jumpsuits sweeping the deck and mopping it first thing in the morning, before a lot of the passengers were even up and about. Dimmie had great respect for people who knew how to work. Sweeping the big wide decks on the ship, well, that looked like work to him. Reminded him of the old women who scurried to sweep the sidewalks before their shops opened, although the ship already looked awfully clean to him. Those sidewalks at home only looked good when they had fresh snow on them.

He would set an alarm and come out on the decks again real early tomorrow. With any luck, they'd be out there sweeping again and maybe they could tell him how to get ahold of the captain. If they spoke English. Dimmie had overheard several crew members chatting, and he didn't understand a word of it. Sounded like their language had a lot of extra letters. But he could try.

If the captain was nice, Dimmie could tell him they had to stop in at Portland, no matter what; he had to catch a bus back to the city. Maybe he could make up an emergency, some kind of family problem. It was a fib, but he had to get off the ship and he'd noticed people turned real soft over a family problem.

He wouldn't mention the murder. It was probably on the captain's mind, but he wasn't going to own up to it.

He would pretend he had nothing to do with it, like the time the police wanted to question everybody about what happened in the Eat Here Diner on Good Friday. There he was, polishing off a stack of pancakes, bothering no one, when somebody threw a fist by the men's room. The menu said they were flapjacks, but they were just plain pancakes. Good ones, though, nice and light, and all he could eat, the menu said. The police made them close the kitchen when they came barreling in after somebody pulled out a pistol and shot up the wall by the pay phone. He never did find out how many he could eat.

The cool air calmed his stomach. Those were good pancakes.

His mouth watered. Maybe he should have taken a slab of that chocolate cake to his cabin. Were people allowed to do that? He'd better wait until breakfast. He didn't want to get in trouble.

Dimmie wiped his hands on his pants and pulled open a heavy outer door, bracing against the wind. It was late and time for bed. Maybe Stu would have left another chocolate on his pillow in his bedroom. *Cabin*: the ship had all kinds of different words.

Chapter thirty-two

Half an hour later, Dimmie had had a nice warm shower, dried his hair, and reconsidered. Why would the captain, the most important man on the whole cruise ship, listen to him? He'd already announced the port was closed, said the ship couldn't stop. How could anybody close a port? The port was made of ocean water, and people can't control the seas. Everybody knows that. Captains must be powerful people.

"Lay low, blend in, be invisible," Brody often said, although how a full-grown man was supposed to be not there at all wasn't real clear to Dimmie. No matter what, he could still see himself. Brody didn't take well to being asked questions. Maybe the captain didn't, either. Talking to him was surely not the way to blend in. He was an important man, after all.

Besides, the captain had announced the police were on their way to the ship. Dimmie had overheard somebody say they would come onboard by a little boat, like the pilot boats in the harbor when they left New York. The captain said people were supposed to cooperate. Dimmie knew that meant the police would be interviewing suspects. Police liked to interview people, although it was just asking a lot of nosy questions, even with that fancy word. With almost two thousand people on the ship, the police wouldn't have time to question them all, not in depth, anyway, especially if they didn't get started until afternoon. Maybe they'd skip Dimmie.

He could blend in better if he wasn't so alone. Maybe he could find Jill and Becky and stay by them. Nobody would question a man with a woman and kid, would they? They could pretend they were a family, just for a little while. He'd like that. Mam said it was bad to get real and pretend mixed up in his mind. Mam wasn't here. If she was, she'd box his ears but good. Still, that wouldn't get him back to the city any faster. He shrugged into clean flannel pajamas. Brody had thought of everything.

The woman's screams invaded his thoughts, no matter what he did to drown out the sound. Any time he wasn't thinking hard about something else, he heard her screaming over and over again like she did in the theatre. The back of his neck knotted up like that dusty macramé planter in Mam's bedroom. Never before had Dimmie considered what killing a mark would do to the man's family and friends. He paced back and forth in the small cabin, back and forth. Swallowing did nothing to ease the knot under his ribs or the shaky panic in his blood. He felt real bad when Da died, and now with the jab of a borrowed steak knife, he'd brought that pain to another person.

Maybe the nuns at school were right. His soul was as black as coal, and he had no right to go on living.

He paced in the small cabin until his bare feet felt raw from the rough carpet. Shortly after eleven-thirty, he'd gone through every option he could think of. He only had one choice.

Chapter thirty-three

The morning of the unplanned sea day passed in freeze-frame motion. The ship's staff did their best to distract passengers with games and activities, but Dimmie wasn't in the mood. The ship was all right, he'd grant that, but not for him. He couldn't put his finger on how he felt, exactly. Something like that time when Aunty Angie got married and made him wear a penguin suit the whole evening. She called it a tuxedo, a mighty fancy word for a girl from the projects. She'd done alright for herself, though, marrying that rich guy with the corner office, at least that's what Mam said.

Dimmie'd had to be on his best behavior the whole time, manners and everything. Mam swatted him for tugging at the straitjacket around his stomach, told him to keep his hands down and a smile on his stupid face. She said it wasn't a straitjacket, it was a cucumber band or something like that. She wasn't the one wearing the infernal thing. A man couldn't even fill his lungs with it on. He didn't feel like himself until he peeled it off late that night.

Aunty Angie's wedding was too fancy schmancy for his taste, and the food wasn't even good. That was usually the best part of any wedding; that and the wedding cake. Sometimes the cake even had those little frosting roses, an explosion of sugar in his mouth if he was lucky enough to get one on his plate. Not this wedding; all they served was dinky dainty foods, better suited to a little girl's tea party. He could have eaten a whole plateful and still not been filled up. And Angie's music was so hoity-toity he couldn't even dance to it, and those who tried looked like little starched pegs on a video game. The cruise brought out the same starchiness in people, from what he could tell.

He craved a footlong, not that fancy food in the dining room. Sometimes a man wanted to dine. He just wanted to *eat*, with a minimum of highbrow manners called for. Maybe if he had a girl to impress; that'd be a different story. A girl on a fancy ship like this would really be something, and he'd use manners the rest of his life if a woman loved him. That would never happen; it wasn't in the cards.

He had planned to hole up in his cabin and block out the world. That worked until somebody kept knocking at his door. He finally gave up and opened it about 10:40am.

"Housekeeping, Mr James-Robert. I go off my shift soon." The room steward shifted on his feet. "May I clean your cabin and make it up for the day?"

"Naw, don't bother, Stu," Dimmie said. "I think I'll just stay in here all day, and the mess don't bother me none."

"My name is Emil, Sir, not Stu. Now, now, you didn't come on a luxury cruise to hide in your stuffy cabin all day, missing out. Have you even had breakfast? If you are feeling unwell, I'd be happy to call room service for you before I take my break."

"No, I don't want to be a bother, or make you work overtime, either. I'll get out of your way." Dimmie reached for his shoes. "I guess I could do with a snack."

"That's the spirit, Sir." Emil stepped into the corridor and returned with a tote bag of cleaning supplies. "It's a fine day for some action on the pool deck. There'll be a barbecue at noon, now that the fog is gone."

Taking Emil's/Stu's advice, Dimmie climbed the stairs to the pool deck. A hundred people or more had the same idea. Some lounged on chairs, others bobbed like corks in the pool, still more sat in the hot tubs that reminded him of a big soup pot. A smile flickered over his lips: passenger soup. Add a few carrots and some noodles.

Having more fun than anybody was Becky, right in the middle of the pool, kicking up a storm. She waved. "Mr Dimmie, watch me! Mommy, are you watching?" She ducked under the water, her pink legs popping up.

Dimmie glanced across the crowded deck for Jill, knowing she'd be nearby. He spotted her and headed her way, dodging a couple of running boys, stopping a few feet from her.

Were those tears? Where was her bright smile?

"Good one, Becky! Do it again!" Jill blotted her nose and called to Becky. "Ah, Dimmie, come sit by me. I could use a friend." She cleared a striped towel off the chair next to hers.

"Jill, are you alright? Are you sad?" He ventured, taking a seat on the green lounge chair. He never knew what to do when Mam cried, but he couldn't walk away when Jill had asked him to sit. Mam usually cried over sad movies, but the big screen over the pool was blank. "What's the matter?"

"Oh, I'm just being silly." Jill waved her hand dismissively. Sniffed. "What are you up to today?"

"No, you're not silly, you're not that kind. If something is making you sad, maybe talking about it will make you feel better." Dimmie dropped into the chair beside her, not sure where those words came from, but recognizing they were exactly what she needed to hear.

She met his eyes under her sun hat. "If you're sure you don't mind…I don't want to keep you from anything…"

He wished he could make her smile. "I have all the time in the world to listen."

"It's just that…I found out…" Jill's blue eyes puddled with tears. She took a shuddering breath. "You see, it's my husband. Becky told you he's serving in the Middle East, and remember I told you I was going to meet him in Portland."

"I remember."

"I had a call late last night. A shore-to-ship message." She blotted a tear. "They said…they said he's been injured. *Shot*." Unbidden, her hand reached for his.

He whispered, "Bad? How bad?" He hated to think of that happy little girl growing up without her dad.

"They said it wasn't *very* bad, a common wound, they said." She hiccupped. "But getting shot in the leg isn't common to *me*. I never knew *anyone* who was shot before, and he's my *husband* and…"

Dimmie nodded, straining to understand. Plenty of men get shot, and a leg wound was nothing. He'd seen worse than that out his own apartment building window. Most likely, the guy would be fine in a little while. Some guys had all the luck. A pretty wife, a cute little daughter, and a war story to go with it. Maybe he'd even get a Purple Heart, like the one Mr Andy kept on that shelf in his apartment at home.

"He's in a hospital in Germany, some place called Landstuhl. The nurse said it took a couple of days to transfer him from the front. They said it wasn't a bad wound, but now he has an infection." Jill's tears tracked down her perfect cheeks, unnoticed. "The nurse who called said they're not sure Theo will make it…they're filling him with antibiotics."

Dimmie squeezed her hand. He knew how quickly a situation could turn on a person. But *Theo?* A guy lucky enough to be Jill's husband had the wimpy name of *Theo?* In the city, he'd have never made it through first grade without getting his nose busted with a name like that.

"Once he's better—and he has to get better! — they'll transfer him to D.C. for another surgery on his leg.

I'm so worried, I can't stand it. I don't know if I should try to get a flight to Germany, or stay on the cruise. They might not let me see Theo, even if I made it there. On the other hand, I don't want Becky to be upset. She's been so excited about this cruise, she even told a grocery clerk about it last week. I'd hate to spoil it for her." She sank back in her chair, her soft hand slipping from Dimmie's grasp. "I can't be with him. I don't even have a way to get word to him. All I can do is pray, and not let Becky see me worry. Of all the times to be stuck on a stupid cruise ship! Walter Reed never seemed so far."

A few silent moments hung in the air as Dimmie scrambled for the right words.

Before he found them, she spoke softly. "I didn't tell Becky about the call, either. To be honest, I wasn't sure she *should* see him, even if we could reach him."

"Her dad? Why not?" Dimmie could swim in Jill's eyes, the same blue as the swimming pool. "And who's this Walter fellow?"

Jill blinked twice. "Walter —?" She giggled, the spell broken. "Oh, you mean Walter *Reed*? That's a big military hospital near Washington, D.C. Theo can get better care there, they said, once he's well enough to travel."

"Mommy, watch this, Mommy! Mr Dimmie, look at me!" Becky's wet pigtails danced. They waved to her and she jumped into the pool.

Dimmie turned back to Jill. "Now, how come you didn't think Becky should see her dad?"

"Well, I debated. You see, she adores her daddy and seeing him like that might upset her. I can't tell her there's a possibility he might... might not..." She sniffed. "Well, it's not good to get a child's hopes up. She's very impressionable."

Dimmie scrolled through his mind. *Impressionable,* like the sign by the big fancy painting on deck six's stairwell? No, that was impressionistic or something.

Her eyes filled again. "What was I thinking, taking my little girl on a cruise when my husband's in a war zone?" She pulled the brim of her sun hat down, her shoulders heaving.

"Mommy, watch me!"

Dimmie patted Jill's hand. "I'll go to her." He walked to the edge of the pool and crouched. "Mommy needs a break, Becky, but I want to watch you. Show me what you got, okay?"

Becky nodded, offered a thumb's up and ducked under the water. She swam across the pool without stopping, calling at the end, "Did you see me, Mr Dimmie? Did you see me?"

Dimmie grinned. "I see you, Becky." What he wouldn't give for a family of his own. That Theo was a lucky man, even if he got shot and might die from the infection or lose his leg or something.

To have the kind of love Jill and Becky had, even for a short time, sounded almost like a reasonable trade off.

Chapter thirty-four

On deck ten, the old man slipped the crewman at his door a fiver, thanked him, and locked the suite's door behind him. Thank goodness for room service. He'd missed dinner and he was hungry. He just couldn't face that loud woman at dinner again. No matter how skillfully he maneuvered to sit at the far end of the table, she managed to finagle her way next to him, even insisting others change places after they were already seated. The ladies in the old neighborhood would have rolled their eyes, called her a brazen hussy or worse. The woman wasn't shy about telling everybody she wanted another husband to add to her collection, and she made no bones about him being her target.

And last night, that other woman in the nightclub, the one who kept giving him the eye, was every bit as bad. She kept dipping her sequined dress strap down and giggling like a floozy. He was too old for that. So was she; what ever happened to a woman having a little dignity? She'd glommed onto him in the lounge the minute he sat down, like she had a homing beacon. He'd hightailed it back to his cabin as soon as she turned away, avoiding the elevators, detouring up three flights of stairs and down a long hall in case she was following him. The last thing he needed was for her to be pounding on his suite door at all hours.

Perched on the tiny sofa, he uncovered the bowl of chicken noodle soup and unwrapped the turkey sandwich.

He eyed the meal dubiously. The soup was not even steaming, the sandwich looked dry, and why on earth would anybody slather whipped cream on a perfectly good brownie? He reached for the remote control, switched on the TV, and switched it off again.

It was just as well he'd decided to skip the show, instead listening to the pianist in the atrium. News of the killing was all over the ship, no matter how hard the staff tried to quash rumors. Not a good time to be in the theatre.

He had spotted the hitman at first glance. He knew the type. When they were on the bus tour in Bar Harbor, he looked closer and remembered the young man from when he was just a runner. Good looking, the boy was, taller now, his face slimmer these days. He still had those ginger waves, although he'd clearly tried to slick them flat with some kind of something.

Several times during the day, he'd tried to talk to James-Robert, maybe remind him who he was without coming right out and introducing himself. He'd even offered him a bite of lobster at lunch.

Dimmie hadn't acted like he recognized him, although they'd met several times when he was just starting out in the business. He'd barely made eye contact, his interest clearly on that other guy, the one who was dead now.

Obviously, he'd been sent; what were the odds of a young hitman randomly going on a cruise? It's not like he was on vacation with the wife and kiddies. Dimmie must have been sent to kill him, although how anybody knew he was onboard was a mystery. Surely the mob had given up trying to track his whereabouts after so long. Maybe he'd been seen in Midtown. Down by the Staten Island Ferry dock; that must have been it. He had often told the younger men when they were just coming up, "If you stand there long enough, the whole world walks by."

But who'd seen him? He'd been careful. Not careful enough, apparently. Must have been one of Jimmy the Deuce's men. Jimmy never let go of anything, and the fact that he was doing life plus a dime didn't help his temper any. Even from the pen, Jimmy kept his contacts alive and functioning like a well-oiled, evil machine. Yes, Jimmy must have told Lucky to put a hit on him. Lucky wasn't bright enough to think of things like that himself. The old man shook his head. The mob wasn't what it used to be.

He pushed aside the tray of food and pulled a beer from the mini-bar. Not as good as the ones on tap in the city, but what's a man to do? He'd outlived his usefulness; no two ways about it. He'd had a good run, but the old code of honor no longer existed. He felt bad for the kids coming up through the ranks these days. All they knew was violence, not like the old days. Sure, the mob did a little extortion and took protection money, some gambling back then. Maybe a little smuggling and gun-running, too, but they built playgrounds for the kiddies in the projects and made sure the little ones had shoes. And the Christmas parties were the best, with a big Christmas tree and toys for everybody, and the *food—!*

A boy growing up in the neighborhood had options back in the old days. Some of them even joined New York's finest or FDNY, following a long line of Irish tradition. Not anymore. The loyalty was gone. Take James-Robert, for instance. He'd been gung-ho, that boy, could have been anybody, but once his father died, well, what choice did he see? All he knew was to join the mob, and keep his mother from finding out. That woman was a tyrant. He'd seen her box her kids' ears right on the street.

Turns out James-Robert was real good at shooting and following orders, bright enough that they could have taught him anything, but that fool Lucky Callahan wasn't one for expanding his talent base. He gave his boys a job and that's all they did until they died, or until Lucky offed them himself, like that young Sean Kennedy.

Colin remembered talking to Sean a few years ago, before the troubles. Sean was in high school at the time, a few years older than James-Robert. He shyly admitted he had dreams of being a big man on campus. He had the smarts for it, too; could have been a real asset to the team, especially in the bookkeeping end of things. Colin would have pushed him to go to one of the colleges in the city, and paid for it, but Lucky would have never allowed that.

A mob boss needed an imagination, and Lucky was as flexible as a concrete sidewalk. Reading between the lines in the day-old newspapers a few months back, he knew young Sean was dead.

So was that man from the bus tour. Stabbed, he'd heard, in the theatre. Seeing the ship on edge over the murder reminded him how fragile life is. Here an innocent man was killed with his wife by his side, and for what? Well, the passengers seemed upset for a little while. Nevertheless, in a short time they were back to dancing and eating and laughing, the murdered man pretty much forgotten. Cruise lines didn't want passengers to have anything but a happy happy experience. Where was the guy's wife now? They'd probably locked her up in her cabin until the ship docked, where her crying couldn't disturb the endless bingo games onboard. People could be so cold.

And now James-Robert's life was as good as over, too. Once Lucky Callahan found out he'd killed the wrong man, it'd be over in hours. The boy never had a chance. He pounded the table, making waves in the soup's greasy sheen. Lucky set the boy up to fail. Sent him to do a hit, but knowing Lucky's impatience, he probably didn't give him enough information to do the job right. And on a cruise ship! How was the boy to know what to do on a cruise ship, when all he knew were the streets of New York? It wasn't right, expecting more of a man than he had to give.

Weighing his options, he bit the sandwich. Not anywhere as good as the ones in any New York deli, but his stomach was uneasy anyway. He'd heard that prisoners on death row had a fancy final meal, their choice, anything under the sun, whatever they wanted. As last suppers go, a dry turkey on white was no great shakes. Had he known how futile life was, he'd have gone to Junior's one last time. Hot pastrami, mustard potato salad, a slab of thick cheesecake…He pushed the brownie across the plate.

With his wife laying in the cold, cold earth, what was the point of living? He had no home, no family, no friends. A few old contacts from decades ago weren't much to go on. He'd outlived his usefulness, like cream gone sour in the refrigerator. Years—no, decades— accruing wisdom and people-skills, and nobody wanted any of it.

He shoved the tray aside. Now what?

Retiring onto a cruise ship had sounded like a good plan. No, it wasn't for him. He'd forgotten how garish they were, and noisy. Piped in music everywhere, people standing around talking, dancing in the hallways, drinking more than enough to lower their inhibitions, if they'd had any when they came onboard. Even taking refuge in the ship's library hadn't helped. Passengers blocked the book shelves, chattering like magpies. Everybody was excited about the next ports, it seemed, but where was the joy without his beloved to share new places with?

He had debated about getting off in Portland, just walking away. To where, he didn't know. Maybe a new start in a nice, peaceful boarding house. Did they still have boarding houses these days? Once the captain announced they'd miss that port, a rock took up residence in his chest. He couldn't bear to be around people another day. Even in his cabin, his room steward bothered him, kept poking his head in to ask if he wanted anything.

Peace and quiet and a reason to go on living, that's all he wanted.

He stepped out onto the balcony. With a shiver, he retreated. Cold out there, and damp, with that heavy fog roiling in the ship's lights. He'd remember to wear his trench coat when he went up on deck. Bad enough to die without a good supper in his belly. He wasn't going to catch a chill in the damp fog.

He jerked toward the bed, certain he'd heard Ellie's tinkling laughter. Once he jumped overboard, maybe he'd see her once again. To hold her one last time would be all the heaven he needed.

Chapter thirty-five

Dimmie shivered, mesmerized, his hands on the icy railing. Water churned in an endless arc behind the massive ship, unconcerned. Who knew there was that much water on the earth, let alone in one spot? How could black water turn into crystalline sparkles at the surface? Light from the half-moon played on the wake. It was a long way down from the open deck to the water's surface. How long would it take? A few seconds? Eternity? Sometimes bad things happened in slow motion, Dimmie knew that. He hoped it wouldn't hurt too bad.

Back when Dimmie was about eight, Sister Mary Michael, his third-grade teacher, led a field trip to the Thomas Jefferson Municipal Pool down on 11thAvenue. They took big yellow school buses. Dimmie had never been in a real swimming pool before, and the blue water looked so soft and clear. As the other kids set down their towels, he made a running dash and hit the water, hard. He came up choking, his neck sore from the impact. As his head spun, cute Jenny McConnell led the pointing and laughing.

Dimmie rubbed his neck, recalling the feeling, as if his head had hit concrete. Maybe jumping overboard wasn't such a good idea. But it had to beat what Lucky Callahan would personally do to him when he found out Dimmie had killed the wrong man, let Kerrick slip through his fingers, and lost his will to kill, all at the same time. Lucky had a mean streak, and he'd take this personally.

How had this happened? He'd never hit the wrong mark before, at least, he didn't think he had. Dimmie never kept records like Sean did; he went where he was told and killed the vic, that was all, making as little mess or noise as possible. Had he ever missed before? No; Lucky would have killed him himself if that had happened, just like he was going to do if Dimmie made it back to the city. He'd been certain the man he'd killed was old man Kerrick, but it wasn't. Just some old nobody on a trip with his wife. His stomach hadn't felt right since the woman started screaming in the theatre. A scream like that had to make her throat sore.

Passengers whispered about the old man, stories taking on a life of their own across the ship. Everywhere he walked onboard, Dimmie had overheard people talking in small groups, speculating on what had happened. On this way to the fantail, he'd overheard murmurs about a heart attack, a fall, was he strangled?

No, he lay dead from a steak knife in the throat, by Dimmie's own hand. He'd heard the dead man's name hissed by passengers in the hallway, the elevator, the stairwell, like a ribbon of sound, choking him, entangling his very soul.

Darren Crandall... Darren Crandall... Darren Crandall...

It was all Lucky Callahan's fault; he should have given Dimmie more to work with. But Lucky wouldn't be the one strung up before he ended up in the East River, and that's if he went easy on him. A single grainy photo from a traffic camera wasn't much to go on. Old guys look all alike, don't they? He didn't have much of a description, either. Irish lilt in his raspy New York voice, wore a fedora, a loudmouth, but secretive — like not even introducing himself at the lobster pound, the place with no dogs at all. The guy's age was right. His wife should have been a clue, but nobody told Dimmie if Kerrick had a wife or didn't. For all he knew, he could have remarried eight times in the intervening years.

Everybody always said Lucky was in a hurry, didn't take time to think things through. The boys didn't have the respect they'd had for old Kerrick, and it made Lucky mad. And now look what he'd done. This was all Lucky's fault, but Lucky would wake up and go on living tomorrow. He'd be angry, probably throw some stuff around his office. In time, he'd have to train a new guy to take his place and Sean's, too, but he'd still be alive and breathing when the sun came up.

And Dimmie wouldn't.

Dimmie tugged the zipper up on his jacket. The chill wind played in his hair; that was one good thing about being dead, he wouldn't have to fight those curls anymore. He'd chosen 12:16 am for several reasons. For one thing, the ship was darkened, especially on the lower open deck, and pretty much deserted. Other evenings, he hadn't seen a soul on this deck. A man needed privacy at a time like this. He guessed a lot of passengers went to bed in their nice cabins, tired from a busy day of playing, their home routines set aside. What would it be like to have a regular job and days off, even vacation time? Other passengers were probably dancing in the lounges; he'd heard the band's drums when he walked by.

He'd miss music most of all. More than the scent of the city, more even than Mam and Gran. There was nothing better than the pulsing beat of the clubs in mid-town, spilling onto a hot summer's night. Lucky didn't let his boys dance, but Dimmie liked watching the women with their sparkly dresses and long hair, smiling with their whitey-white teeth, moving to the music's rhythm. Music was going to be a loss.

And pizza; he'd miss pizza. A folded slice was heaven, and the kind that came with extra napkins was the best. You knew it was going to be good if they gave you extra napkins without even having to ask. Hot and greasy, dripping stringy cheese. The best. He'd miss pizza.

And the subway. He'd miss the subway. Something about walking down those grimy stairs to the city's underworld felt like magic, like entering another world, leaving the bright city streets behind. He never knew if there'd be a street performer that day or not. Some of them were really good. Last month, a guy was dressed up like the Statue of Liberty, standing perfectly still, bowing when somebody threw coins in his jar, then freezing in place like he was made of marble again. Not even blinking. How did he do that?

And that guy with the drums. Months ago, but he could still feel the pulsing rhythm in his blood when he thought about it. Boy, was Lucky mad; staying to watch the drummer made Dimmie late to a meeting about some guy with the fancy briefcase. He wouldn't miss Lucky one bit.

A few times he'd stopped to watch a fight down on the subway platform, and that was good, too, like the fights on Friday nights on TV, only without the ring. The One train was like a part of his home; he'd ridden it alone since he was seven years old, and he was as comfortable on it as in his own living room. More comfortable, maybe. Sometimes he put his feet up on the nearby seat if it wasn't too crowded. Mam wouldn't tolerate that at home.

People-watching; he'd miss that too, seeing all of humanity moving through the crowded New York streets in a never-ending wave. Yes, New Yorkers were known for being rude, but he didn't see it like that. Mostly, they had places to be and other people got in their way. You can't blame them, really. People were funny things.

Once a family of tourists even asked him for directions. They wanted to know where 34th street was, not knowing they were already right there at Penn Station. He asked where they were from, and they said Vancouver. He couldn't have been more pleased had they said Mars. He tried to tell Mam about it later on, but she turned away and said what was the point of talking to anybody from outside the city? No good could come of it, people like that. He'd miss people, the way they talked and moved and laughed and all.

He'd miss Jill and little Becky and the family he'd never have. He would have been a good father, like Da, only now he'd never get the chance. He pushed that thought aside. Thinking about all the things he'd miss wasn't helping. He had no choice, and that was that.

The most important reason he chose the time of his death was that 12:16 wasn't divisible by five. Dimmie hated the times tables, all of them, but fives most of all. He could still hear Sister Mary Paul chanting, "*One* times five is *five*. *Two* times five is *ten*. *Three* times five is—" Well, he didn't care what five times anything was, and it was already 12:03. He wasn't going to spend his last few minutes on earth working a math problem, but he knew he didn't have much time left.

Dimmie closed his eyes, one hand on the cold railing. Looking at the rushing water made his stomach feel funny, like when he ate too much cabbage. Like a wrung-out dishrag. That was one thing he wasn't going to miss, washing dishes after dinner. Mam made up every excuse in the book to get out taking her turn washing up. Taking her own sweet time in the bathroom, complaining about a broken fingernail or wet nail polish, saying she had to make a phone call right this minute. Well, who'd do it now, huh?

He stared at the second hand on his watch, willing it to slow down, to speed up, to freeze in place.

Chapter thirty-six

"James-Robert, my boy, is that you? What on earth are you doing out here?" The old man's voice crackled in the dark. "Run along, boy, I have something to take care of."

Dimmie startled, his heart in his mouth. *Something to take care of...* How many times had he heard Colin Kerrick say that in the same gruff voice? He opened his eyes. "You?"

His mind swam. How could the nice old man who'd shared his lobster in Bar Harbor have turned into Colin Kerrick? Wearing his familiar trench coat and fedora, Dimmie recognized him as surely as if they'd never parted. The authoritative voice, the coat, a whiff of Old Spice...

He told himself sternly, *It's one of those tricks your mind plays on you. You've never tried to kill yourself before, so who knows what happens right before? It can't be the old Boss.*

"Run along, I said. I need to take care of something. I picked out this time and place, and you can't be here."

Dimmie blinked at the stern voice. With a shudder, he glanced at his watch one last time and drew himself to his full five-nine. "No, I was here first. I'm gonna jump off the back of this ship at 12:16, and you can get outta my way."

"What's that you say, aye? *You're* going to jump?"

"That's what I said, ain't it?" Dimmie's voice faltered. "I messed up, Boss. Lucky Callahan sent me to off you, and I hit the wrong man. I killed a nice old man with a wife and the scream she let out…I keep hearing her screaming and screaming…I can't go on living anymore."

The old mob boss leaned closer, his voice softer. "So, you decided to jump. Take the easy way out, aye?"

"I got no choice." Dimmie gulped. "You know better than anybody what Lucky will do to me if I go home. I got nothing to live for no more. It's nighttime; no one will ever find me in the dark." He glanced at the inky water. With the moon behind a cloud, he could hear the ship's wake, but the dark water below reflected no light. Would it hurt when he hit the surface? Maybe if he tucked his head, rolled up like a ball…Well, the pain wouldn't last long.

"I understand you're in a bind, my boy, but let me tell you a little something before you jump." Colin Kerrick took Dimmie's arm and pulled him toward a teak bench. "What's your hurry? You think Saint Peter's eager to have you show up?"

Dimmie flinched. He'd forgotten about Saint Peter waiting at the Pearly Gates. Surely, hell gaped wide open for souls like his, like the nuns warned the boys at Saint Margaret's. The Reverend Mother told him his soul was as black as coal for breaking Erna's new pencil, and he'd done a lot worse than that in the years since then. He slowly sank onto the bench.

"Want a peppermint?" Colin pulled one from his pocket, their hands grazing as Dimmie reached for it. A whiff of Old Spice clung to the old man.

Dimmie recoiled. "Boss, I…"

"No, you let me do the talking. You sit there and listen to me; do you hear me?" Colin's voice brooked no argument.

How many times had Dimmie heard Lucky use that same phrase? It must be what all mob bosses say.

"You can't take your life. You're young, you have years ahead of you." Colin settled back. "I always hated hearing the boys call you dim wit. Everybody, even your own mother. You have a good heart, and you could be anybody. Me, on the other hand…you see, my wife died not long ago. Ellie was my reason for living. What have I got to live for? I need you to get out of my way, and don't go hollering 'Man Overboard' after I climb over the rail, you hear me?"

"You? No, Boss, you're mixed up." Dimmie shook his head. "I'm the one who's gonna jump into the water, not you. I'm gonna die tonight. You're trying to confuse me. I—"

"You want to die, my boy, leave everything behind? Just erase yourself, like you never existed?"The old man's voice softened in the night air. "Why would you think such a thing?"

"I don't want to die, but I got no choice. I…I really messed up bad this time. I can't get that woman's crying out of my head. I can't make it right." The splash of water two decks below filled the silence. "Why are *you* planning to jump? I don't want you to jump, Boss. You're the only one who ever made me feel like I could do anything right, after Da went to heaven. Maybe if I had a father…"

"Your dad was a good man, worked hard. I knew him well, and he loved you. I'm sure he was sad, knowing he wouldn't be here to raise you right." He remembered when Dimmie's father was killed in that accident, leaving a hole in Dimmie's little boy heart that never quite healed. He'd watched the boy give up trying anymore.

"What happened to you, Mr Colin?" Dimmie ventured. "I heard you went into the Witness Protection program, and nobody heard anything anymore. I thought that was supposed to be a sweet deal."

"Beats prison, I guess, but I'm lonely and I'm bored. Ellie was my reason for living. I even looked into one of those places where old folks go to die. Not for me." Colin shifted on the teak bench. "Chilly out here. That's why I came on this cruise, to see if I'd enjoy living on a cruise ship all the time. Cost a lot less than those places and the food is better."

"I like the food just fine here. Would they really let you stay on the ship? I thought everybody had to get off at the end of the cruise."

Colin chuckled. "If you pay people enough, they let you do just about anything. I was going to book another cruise after this one, back to back, they call it, and keep on going. It's not for me. I can't stand the way those ladies look at me. They bat their eyes and one even called me I spent too many years making my way in the world to be *cute.*"

He sobered. "My life was a good one, James-Robert. I did some bad things, aye, but a lot more good ones. I married a fine woman and made a home. I led men and I taught them some things. I had a good run, but the old ways are gone and I'm just a useless old man. I lived a code of honor that doesn't exist anymore. You, on the other hand, James-Robert, you have your whole life ahead of you."

They sat silently, the darkness broken only by the wan light from a distant ship's light around the corner.

"Gran always says God sends angels to people where they're needed. Maybe you—No, I have to jump." Dimmie's voice wobbled in the night air. "I can't go back. I don't have it in me to face Lucky Callahan and the boys. The captain said the police will interview people. I'm trapped. Either I go to jail when they figure it was me who stabbed that man, or Lucky finds out I didn't kill you and it's the cement boots for me. Worse, maybe." He sniffed and stood. "My life is as good as over. I have to jump. Do you think it'll hurt when I hit the water?"

"What's your hurry?"

Chapter thirty-seven

Lost in his own thoughts, Dimmie moved to the rail, while Colin sat on the bench.

Finally, Colin mused, "Your dad missed out. I never had kids of my own, nobody to guide and teach. I always wanted to have a son, to be a father to somebody. Do you think it's too late for me to take a stab at that job?''

"Being a dad?" Dimmie cocked his head. "Mr Kerrick, you're pretty old. And how are you going to have a baby without a wife?"

"I had a wife, the best. Someday, you'll find a woman to love you like my Ellie loved me. I promise you that."The old man straightened. "James-Robert, I have an idea. Do you know how to cook, my boy?"

"Cook?" Dimmie puzzled. "Yeah, I do all the cooking at home. I watch those shows on TV and try things out. Gran said she's too old to think of what to make and Mam never was a good cook. She burns everything. Turns the burner on high and goes to watch the TV until the smoke detector goes off. Then she says it's done." Dimmie turned from the rail. "What do you care if I can cook?"

"I'm a terrible cook, and that's the honest truth. If you'd be willing to keep us fed, I can do the rest." Colin slapped his knee. "Helping you get a fresh start might be just the thing I need to go on. What do you think, my boy, if we both face a few more years of living? Together, I mean. You and I can go somewhere, anywhere. It's a big wide world outside the city, and it's beautiful. A new life will do us both good."

"Me and you? Together?"

Dimmie glanced at his watch. *Two minutes.* "Outside the city? But, why?"

"Think about it. A new beginning. With my Ellie gone, I'm bored. I'd enjoy your company. You can be my reason for living, and I can teach you a thing or two. Ever since you were a little boy, I've had my eye on you, knew you were somebody special. Maybe the angels sent *you* to *me*." Colin stood and took Dimmie's arm. "Come on, my boy. Walk with me. We have to figure out tomorrow. We need a plan." His heart pounded. A plan! He hadn't felt this alive since…well, since Ellie died.

Dimmie glanced one last time at the churning water below. "But, I was going to—"

"— and now, you're not. Let's figure out a way to get you past the police in the morning, and we'll sort out the rest later on. Aye?"

"I'm scared, Mr Kerrick. Say we get me off the ship. Lucky Callahan will track me down, you know he will. I don't want to be looking over my shoulder the rest of my life."

"Nah, I'm still faster and smarter than Lucky, even at this age. He's just…lucky. He can't even run his own life. He's done running yours. I'm thinking we'll put you in a hotel in Halifax until we can get you a new name. A new passport, too."

"We'd need a guy. You know a guy, Mr Kerrick?"

"I know a guy. I know guys everywhere, James-Robert. I'll make some calls in the morning. We'll get you off the ship safe and sound. Don't think any more about it because—''

"— I'm not very good at it," Dimmie finished.

"Oh, yes, you are. You're much smarter than you think, and quick on your feet, too. I was going to say, don't bother thinking because I have an idea and I'm sure it'll work." He chuckled in the dim light. "This feels like the old days. You'll get a new start, and I'll be right beside you."

"Boss, I …I want to thank you, but the words ain't coming." Dimmie wiped his eyes with a sleeve.

In the dark, the young man stepped into the old man's outstretched arms, breathing in the scent of Old Spice and peppermint.

Is that what his new life smelled like?

Chapter thirty-eight

In cabin 507, Dimmie sat on his bed, thinking harder than he'd ever thought about anything before. Until now, he'd pretty much focused on the job. Lucky told him who to kill, and he did it without a second thought. Well, he thought about it plenty, felt sick every time, but he obeyed. What choice did he have?

Now he had every choice in the world before him, Mr Kerrick said so, and his mind reeled. He unwrapped the chocolate Stu had left on his pillow, letting it melt in his mouth. He slipped between the fresh sheets, with nobody telling him to brush his teeth or turn off the light or even hang up his shirt, the one he'd left draped on the chair. He'd left his socks on the floor, too. Nobody could tell him what to do anymore.

Maybe they should have thrown one of those life rings over the side of the ship; let the crew think somebody went overboard, give him more of a running start. Nobody would think to chase a man who fell off a ship into the ocean, would they? No: Stu would notice his bed had been slept in, and surely the officers would ask a room steward what he knew. From what Dimmie could tell, Stu knew a lot.

Stu had a way of showing up in Dimmie's cabin, folding his clothes, wiping the counter. He'd even left a dish of prunes on the desk with a note. "Hope you feel better soon — Emil." He didn't know why he signed his name Emil when he'd said his name was Steward that first day. Anyway, that was a joke; Dimmie had refolded the toilet paper into a little pointy triangle after he made a stinky. He guessed Stu thought he was plugged up, like Gran got sometimes after she ate too much cheese. Gran sure was cranky when that happened.

Maybe if Colin said they should throw one of those white life rings in the ocean, he could have slept on one of those big lounge chairs on the pool deck. No; when would he ever get the chance to have a nice cabin like this again, and all to himself? He wasn't going to waste the opportunity, and besides, it was too late now. Mr Kerrick was probably in bed long ago.

And Colin said he had a plan. One sure way to mess up a plan was to mix it up it halfway through. Sean called that "changing horses mid-stream," but Dimmie didn't think he knew any more about horses than he did. Which wasn't much.

After he and Colin made a new home someplace, would he be able to see a real horse, maybe even ride one? Later on, when he found a wife and had some kiddies, he'd take them to ride a pony. He'd seen ponies on the television, and they looked gentle. A little girl would enjoy that.

Knowing he'd never see Mam or Gran again, a cold feeling like those raw oysters in the sports bar settled below his ribs.

I'll never see them no more if Lucky gets ahold of me, either. This way, they won't have to have a funeral or anything. I'll be gone like I never was here in the first place.

But I won't be dead.

He stared at the ceiling, rolling Kerrick's words over and over in his mind. There on the darkened deck, before they parted at the elevator bank, the old man's voice took on new energy.

"You can finally have a life, James-Robert, a life of your own making. That's what's great about America. That's why our families came from the Old Country. You can do anything you want, be anybody you want. Nobody will tell you what to do ever again." He clapped his hand on Dimmie's shoulder. What *do* you like to do, my boy?"

Dimmie stared at his shoes. People told him what to do all the time, but no one ever asked what he wanted. He said slowly, "I like cars. I like watching them. Some of them are really fast."

"Cars? We'll get you your own car. You can pick the color. You can learn to drive, aye." Kerrick snapped his fingers. "You can learn about engines, go to mechanics school if you want, or even college. You'll need new papers; piece of cake. We could set you up in your own business. You'd be good at that. You'd be good at a lot of things, my boy. Why, you can even find a nice wife, make a houseful of ginger-headed babies." He smiled. "I noticed you watching that little girl and her mother."

Dimmie's shoulders relaxed. A little girl like Becky would be a joy. That smile of hers, even with two teeth missing, charmed him. He was silent for a long minute.

"No more hits?" Dimmie ventured a sideways glance. "I don't want to do no more hits."

"Never again."

"Do you think I could play poker?"

"My boy, the opportunities are endless. Wherever we go, I guarantee there'll be somebody just waiting for you to take your place at the poker table." Colin chuckled. "And I'll be right beside you."

Chapter thirty-nine

Half the night, Dimmie wrote and wrote on the yellow legal pad Colin gave him. The other half of the night, he lay sleepless in his bed, the cabin walls pushing in on his thoughts. Twice, he jumped up to add another note. Had he written enough to lead the Feds to Lucky? All the hits he could remember, the heists, the protection money, names and dates and places. Colin said to write it all down and fold the paper into one of the ship's logo envelopes in the desk drawer. Implicate, that's what he said.

"Our new run is just beginning," the old man said, "And it's time Lucky's came to an end. You'll give the Feds enough cold cases to keep them busy for years."

"Jerk a knot in his tail," Dimmie agreed. Brody would move up in the mob, and Brody was a fair man. Lucky's temper could explode in prison without hurting anybody.

The ship's fog horn sounded every minute and a half. He debated about going out on the open deck to see if the fog showed any sign of letting up, but he was more sleepy than curious. And the smooth bedsheets were so comfortable. Would his new home have soft sheets? Tired or not, his thoughts raced like the old wooden roller coaster at Coney Island. Up, down, around again. Colin had assured him he had a plan, but trust didn't come easily for him. Still, he was alive, and that was more than he'd planned on being.

Could they really get off the ship without getting caught? The police were bent on interviewing everybody; they were like pit bulls when it came to not letting go. He'd have to lay low today, Colin said, act normal, and he assured him he could do it. He just had to get through this extra unplanned sea day like nothing had happened, and tomorrow, they'd get off in Halifax and start their new life. Together, like father and son.

One more day.

He and Colin had parted at the aft elevator bank as the ship's nightclub was closing. Passengers passed Dimmie in the hallway, some weaving from the motion of the ship, others still clutching their beer glasses. Waiting for the elevator, conversations centered on the attack on that poor passenger. Dimmie kept his head down. He was pretty sure no one had noticed him in the theatre; the audience's attention had been on the performers when he stabbed the man. Still, you never know; what if somebody ratted him out to the police in the morning? Could Colin really get him to a place where he could live his life without feeling like he was one step ahead of being found out?

About ten to six, he gave up trying to sleep. He shook the wrinkles out of his shirt, slipped on his grey pants and shoes and made his way through the silent ship to deck fourteen, the buffet. Watching the endless sea below him would take him mind off the problems, and maybe some food would calm his stomach. It felt like little balls were rolling around in there. Spiky balls. Made of ice. With rocks in them, like the boys made to throw at the first snowfall every year.

Exiting the elevator, Dimmie glanced out the floor to ceiling windows. Had the fog lifted yet? He froze. For a second, it felt like somebody invisible was squeezing his heart. The fog had lessened, replaced by a weak rain. The lights of a big city twinkled through the lines of water trailing down the glass. Halifax was only a mid-sized place, a small city at best. He promised he'd keep Dimmie safe, away from the small Russian mob who called it home.

This was no small city. Tall buildings glinted their lights across the water. Tiny boats, fishing boats and lobster boats and sailboats, bobbed in the harbor, waiting for dawn to break, blurring in the misty wisps of fog. Dimmie stared across the harbor. Oddly familiar, it seemed; where had he seen this place before? *Postcards.* A chill ran down his spine like ice water.

He'd seen this scene on postcards in the little shop in Bar Harbor, with "Boston" scrawled across the top of each card. How could this be Boston? The captain said the ship was going to Halifax, and today was supposed to be a sea day. The *Ocean Serenity* maneuvered relentlessly closer to a long pier, closer and closer. He squinted to make out the large red letters lit above the pier.

CRUISEPORT BOSTON

Chapter forty

Sweat broke out on Dimmie's brow. He turned to run. Somewhere. Anywhere. Colin Kerrick had said he'd keep him safe in Halifax, but Boston was a different story. He had to get to Colin, but he didn't even know his cabin number. Turning, he bumped into a woman in a white uniform.

"Sorry, I—"

"Good morning, Sir. Early breakfast today? Quite a surprise out the window, don't you think?"

"I…uh…it…"

She went on, seeming to not notice his discomfiture. "Captain made the call in the night to turn into Boston. Put the pedal to the metal. It's closer than Nova Scotia, and…I don't know if you heard…there was an *incident* onboard last night. That's what the brass said to call it. I guess Captain figured he could deal with American police better than Canadian authorities." She flashed a grin. "Although those red costumes the Mounties wear are something to see. I do love a man in a uniform." She shook herself. "Excuse me, Sir, I shouldn't be chattering on. We're supposed to stop rumors, they said in our stand-up meeting. I'm sure you want your morning coffee. Take a seat and I'll pour you a cup." She stepped behind the wait station, greeting a fellow crew member.

Dimmie sank into a chair, heedless of the few other passengers scattered throughout the dining area and the staff bustling behind the buffet counters. Even the aroma of steaming coffee didn't penetrate his gloom.

Boston! Could Colin get him off the ship in Boston? He strained to remember which gangs owned Beantown. Did Colin have any old contacts here? Would they still talk to him after so long?

He watched a jet dip toward the harbor, pulling up at the last moment, landing on a runway lit by rows of tiny lights, white, then yellow. Where had the plane come from? Lucky people, whoever they were, being able to fly around like that. What he wouldn't give to get away from the mess he'd created on earth. From that height, the earth had no troubles at all.

Not like here. He should have jumped overboard when he had the chance. If he jumped now, in broad daylight, somebody would be sure to rescue him, and that's the last thing he needed. Probably one of those little lobster boats. He shuddered; he'd seen enough lobster to last a lifetime, if he had a lifetime ahead of him.

Someone slid a plate of jam-filled pastries in front of him, but he didn't lift his head. "I ain't hungry anymore."

"Sure, and you must eat, my boy. You have an adventure ahead, and a man can't work on an empty stomach." Colin clapped him on the shoulder and slid into the chair across the table.

"You? You're awfully chipper this morning," Dimmie groused. "Didn't you see where we are?"

"I watched the ship pull into the harbor from my balcony. I was hoping I'd find you here before you got yourself all upset, aye. I know how you like to eat. No need to worry, my boy. I was on my phone during the night. Called in a few favors owed me. Boston is Irish, you know." Colin smiled. "Go get yourself a proper breakfast, bring me a roll, and I'll tell you all about it. One of those soft rolls, not the hard ones. I don't like crumbs on my shirt."

Dimmie loaded his plate with scrambled eggs, fried potatoes, and a heap of bacon, more bacon than Mam would let him eat in a month. His mind raced. Was it really going to be okay? He snagged two soft rolls for Colin and headed back to the table.

A few minutes later, Dimmie wiped his lips with a napkin, his stomach and heart full. Colin had really come through for him; they just had to put the plan in place. As they ate, Colin explained in a low voice what he'd set up in the night. He'd booked a hotel for Dimmie; the trick was going to be getting him off the ship before the police questioned the passengers. There was a slight chance somebody could identify him from the theater, even if they hadn't seen him kill that man.

"You did some acting in high school, didn't you, James-Robert?"

"That's a funny question."

"And one needing an answer, aye."

"Not really." Dimmie set his cup down. "I was the Tin Man one time, but that was about it. Sister Mary Michael wanted me to act more, said it would give me confidence, but mostly I helped paint the scenery and watched from the back of the stage during the plays. Why?"

"Today, you're going to use everything you ever learned from watching those actors, and everything you've seen on television, too." Colin buttered his roll. "You're going to act like one of the ship's officers, confident, a leader, and you're going to bluff your way right through the police line. Once you're onshore, you're home free."

Dimmie dropped his fork. "How'm I going to do all that? You know my job; I try *not* to be seen. I don't know if I —"

"First off, you're not a hitman anymore, remember?" Colin smiled, his voice low. "I know you got this in you, my boy. Let me tell you what you're going to do…."

Before they finished breakfast, the captain's voice came over the broadcast system. Sure enough, the Boston police would be boarding the *Ocean Serenity* within a few minutes, and intended to interview each passenger in a tent they'd set up on the pier.

"Since we are not cleared to port in Boston until Tuesday, we cannot disembark passengers outside of the port itself. Please follow instructions when your deck is called for interviews. We'll get these done as quickly as possible and be on our way to beautiful Halifax by this afternoon."

Colin sat back in his chair. "See, my boy, it's just as I told you. They'll march passengers off, ask them if they know anything, and march them back on again."

"Do you really think this'll work?"

"Not a doubt in my mind." Colin winked. "You and me, we're going to walk off and keep on going. Trust me."

"I trust you." Dimmie's hand shook, sending little waves across his water glass. "I have to, don't I?"

"That you do, my boy. Now, remember, do what I said to do on deck two, then meet me in my suite with that paper you wrote in the night. As soon as they call for the second group to talk to the police, my corridor will be hectic enough for you to blend in. Don't carry anything with you, not even that fancy new passport Lucky's boys made for you. That man, he's gone. By bedtime, you'll be a new man."

"You really think I can do this?"

The older man shook the younger one's hand. "I have every faith in you, my boy."

Chapter forty-one

Back in his cabin, Dimmie changed into the dark
clothing Colin told him to wear. Good thing Brody had
bought navy shirt and trousers. With any luck, no one
would notice it wasn't a crew uniform. People never really
look at one another, Colin said, and at a glance, he'd be
fine. His hand shook as he buttoned the shirt. He placed his
wallet on the nightstand, slipped the envelope into his
pocket and nodded approval in the mirror. Too bad he had
to leave; the cabin was a decent one, and Stu took good
care of him. He'd never had a room to himself before.
Sharing a room with Gran was no great shakes. He
wouldn't miss her snoring. For a little old lady, she had the
chops of a jack hammer.

On his way to deck two, Dimmie paused to listen to
more announcements. As Colin had surmised, passengers
would be interviewed by the police in that big white tent
the police set up on the pier. They would be called to the
theatre by deck number, then sorted by cabin numbers. The
captain sternly said no one would be exempt; like the
muster drill, it was mandatory.

Once the elevator opened on deck two, Dimmie
glanced both ways, turned right, disregarding the Crew
Only Beyond This Point sign, then hurried down the
uncarpeted staircase to his left. The lower deck was purely
utilitarian; no glitz and glitter here. He wouldn't be here
long.

Colin told him over breakfast he'd pulled up a map of the ship's layout on his laptop during the night, and he'd been right so far. Dimmie strode down the long crew corridor, staying close to the wall. Colin said the crew called it I-75 and he was pretty sure there were no security cameras in this part of it. *Pretty sure*—was that good enough? Dimmie read the signs on the heavy metal doors as he passed by: Utilities. Electrical. Storage. Danger: High Voltage. *Laundry.*

He glanced over his shoulder, his heart thundering. He slowly pushed open the heavy metal door. A wave of steam hit his face like a sauna. He'd never seen a real sauna; he'd planned to check out the one in the ship's spa, but he spent that time talking with Jill instead. It was time well spent, but the humid laundry facility still made him think of what a sauna would feel like. Maybe Mr Kerrick knew about saunas. Who knows, maybe he'd even take Dimmie to one once they found a new home.

"The world is waiting for you," Colin had repeated. "You can do anything you want, once we get through today. You'll need a new name. Be thinking of what you'd like to be called."

Joseph. Martin. Hank. Dimmie pushed the random thoughts away. He had a job to do and he meant to do it, not let Colin down. Colin had said only four crew members worked in the massive laundry at any given time. How he knew all that, Dimmie didn't know. Maybe he'd taken the VIP ship's tour the first day. That would have been something; the brochure said they went into the crew areas and behind the theatre, even the galleys, where all that food came from. Maybe he could have seen the ess cargo he'd accidentally ordered for dinner that first night. Did the cooks keep the snails in a tank of water, like the little fish at Hobson's Pet Shoppe at home? He'd have to remember to ask Kerrick about it later on.

Focus, time to focus.

Across the steamy laundry, two women pulled stacks of bedding from a long folding machine, piling it on rolling racks, not bothering to speak over the noise. Another dragged a bin full of striped pool towels to an elevator. Dimmie edged to the left, keeping a wary eye out for the other worker. There were supposed to be four of them. Where was the other one?

He spotted the officer's uniforms on a rack, hanging right where Colin said they'd be. He snagged two sets, bundled in clear plastic like they'd come from the dry cleaner's on 33rd. He grabbed another, just in case: he wasn't sure what size old man Kerrick wore. The old boss wasn't big, but he seemed to increase in size when he spoke. Draping them over his arm, Dimmie slipped out into the corridor.

"Hey, man, what you got there?" A man in a black shirt and pants stopped, his wheeled cart's wheels squeaking in protest.

Dimmie froze. "I—"

"Those guests in the penthouse keep calling about their laundry being late. I was coming to take it to them, but since you're here, move it along, will you?" Frowning as his beeper sounded again, the man indicated a table beside the door. Wicker baskets with folded clothing nestled on white tissue paper waited, each with a paper tag on top. "That's theirs, the one on the corner," and he hurried down I-75 without a backwards glance.

Dimmie drew a full breath and made his way to the staircase. The penthouse people would have to wait. He wasn't a delivery boy, and he was done taking orders from everybody. He'd follow Colin's plan, then figure out how to live his own life on his own terms. Once he'd changed in Colin's suite, the next phase of the plan would fall into place. Colin had full confidence, he said.

Unless old man Kerrick set him up; for all he knew, the police could be onto him already, waiting for him to make a false move so they could nab him. Would handcuffs hurt? He'd seen enough men with their hands behind their backs, the uniformed police stuffing them into squad cars. Were the police waiting for him? What was worse, being arrested for murder or facing Lucky at home? No—neither was in the cards, not today, not for him.

Don't think, don't think, don't think, he chanted in his mind like he did before a hit. He slowed his breathing, counting two seconds. In, two counts, hold, two counts, out, hold, in. Once he had a plan worked out, the worst thing he could do was second-guess himself halfway through.

Even if Kerrick's plan failed, he'd already had another night and morning alive, and that was something.

Chapter forty-two

Dimmie tapped on Colin's suite, then pressed the doorbell button for good measure. His own inside cabin had no doorbell. Colin opened the door and pulled Dimmie in by the arm. "No need to slink around out there, James-Robert, come in, come in. Let me see what you have there, aye?"

After checking the uniforms Dimmie had over his arm, Colin pronounced them "perfect for the task at hand," and sent Dimmie to try on the one with two stripes on the sleeves. The suite boasted two bathrooms, more than one old man needed, unless he made a stinky, James-Robert guessed. How many times had he wished his apartment had two bathrooms? Never mind the stinkies; waiting for Mam and Gran was hard enough. He never knew what they were doing in there that took so long. Himself, he could go and be out in under two minutes, less if he skipped washing his hands. He'd ask Colin about it; maybe their new home, wherever it was, could have two bathrooms. Imagine, one all to himself. And a big window, so he could watch the birds. Would their new home have birds to look at?

As he pulled up the uniform trousers and buttoned the jacket, he called to Colin, "Fancy digs you got here. Any chance of us ever going on another cruise, like a vacation, huh?"

"One day at a time, my boy. Let me see how you look."

Dimmie tugged at the collar as he stepped back into the suite. Catching sight of his reflection in the full-length mirror, he grinned. Mam always said, "Clothes make the man." If she could see him now, maybe she'd use his given name for once.

Colin smoothed Dimmie's tie and nodded. "You look fine, my boy, confident and all. Even taller. Did you hear the loudspeaker while you were dressing? Called deck three passengers to the theater. Get on your way now. Nobody will stop an officer."

Dimmie straightened his cap and glanced at Mr Kerrick one last time. Their eyes met, and the old man caught the younger one in a long hug. Without a word, Colin flashed a thumbs up, and Dimmie stepped into the wide corridor.

Walk briskly, he told himself. *If I'm going to get caught, I may as well go out boldly.*

Briskly, boldly. Those were Sister Mary Michael's words. She encouraged Dimmie repeatedly to "Live your life boldly; don't let anyone tell you what to do." Well, his days of being told what to do were over; Mr Kerrick said so.

A man asked him near the elevator bank, "You're the second officer, right? My wife here is scared. Tell her it'll be okay, will you?"

Dimmie ducked his head. *Acting,* he reminded himself, *"What would an officer do?"* and drew himself up to his full height. "Nothing to worry about, Ma'am. Just answer what the police ask and you'll be back onboard in no time."

He felt guilty for play-acting — How many times had Mam scolded him for getting real and pretend mixed up? — but smiled as the woman visibly relaxed. Not wanting to risk another conversation, he sidestepped the swarm of passengers waiting for the elevator and hurried down the nearby staircase to the theater's main level.

A line of passengers stretched out into the corridor. Dimmie moved to the end of the line, then remembered his role. *An officer never waits in lines, they don't wait for anything, they're in charge, mind,* Colin told him. Remembering his manners, he pressed past the line, repeating, "Excuse me" so people would move out of his way. And move they did, every one of them, without hesitation, at a glance at his uniform.

"Sheep," Lucky Callahan would call them; people who moved mindlessly, putting one foot in front of the other, doing as they were told like dumb herded animals. How many times had Lucky called the New York tourists sheep? Especially the ones on those open-top tour buses, with their cameras and wide eyes, necks craning up at the skyscrapers. Well, sheep suited Dimmie's purposes just fine. He just had to hope the police officers were as mindless.

Not likely.

Once in the theatre, he paused, scanning the lay of the place. With the bright house lights on, the magic of the evening shows was absent. Out of the corner of his eye, he noticed the place where he'd stabbed Darren was still cordoned off with those red velvet ropes like the movie house used. He turned away; that was another time, another life, another person. Dimmie the hitman was gone. Gone forever, and not coming back. James-Robert was on the move.

Crew members directed passengers to fill in the rows in the center section while others consulted clipboards by the exit doors on the floor level. Colin said they'd most likely be upper level staff, but by their crew shirts, Dimmie knew Colin guessed wrong. These people looked more like bar staff or activities crew. Well, if that was the worst thing he'd got wrong, it was okay. Everybody made mistakes.

Averting his face so no crew member could recognize him, or more importantly, know he wasn't the man whose uniform he wore, he made his way toward the stage at the bottom of the theatre. The Emergency Exit door, stage left, was propped open a few inches, just waiting for him. Could it be that easy?

Chapter forty-three

From Colin's balcony, they'd seen the large white tent on the pier with its mouth gaped wide, slowing chewing the line of passengers waiting to enter, some on the gangway, others on the pier itself. Two uniformed police officers directed them into the tent, a handful at a time. Two others led the passengers out the back of the big tent and toward the midships gangway. Dimmie had counted six police cars, plus two staters parked to the left. Colin said because the incident happened at sea, there'd be feds in the mix, but they hadn't identified which ones they were. It was hard to see their badges from that height, and Colin said using his binoculars would be a dead giveaway.

A young woman in an Activities Staff shirt called for passengers from deck five to follow her down the aisle and fill in the rows on the right-hand side, upper section. A string of passengers followed like kindergarteners.

Staticky, a voice came over the theater sound system, thanking people for their patience, assuring them there was just a slight delay but they'd be on their way quickly. Sternly, "We remind you, it is imperative you tell the police anything you may have seen surrounding the incident, no matter how inconsequential it seems."

A couple of young women stood up from their seats midway down the aisle. "I'm not sitting here wasting any more time. I'm on *vacation*, you know!" one complained.

A few passengers nearby joined in. "Yeah, they can't keep us hostage like this. Let them solve their own crime without me. They can't tell us what to do. Come on, let's see if the pool bar is open."

Dimmie glanced down the aisle. No crew members were near enough to hear the murmuring. He'd used uneasy crowds to cover his hits often enough to know that when one person stirred things up, others were bound to follow. Right now, he needed order, not people running around on their own. Time for those old acting skills. What would an officer do? Take charge. Colin had said no one would question a person in an officer's uniform.

He walked down the aisle and spoke firmly. "You need to take your seats, all of you."

Without hesitation, every one of the passengers obeyed. Several said, "Yes, Sir, sorry."

Hiding a grin, Dimmie moved down the aisle. Why hadn't he ever thought to borrow a uniform of some kind before now? Those people dropped into their seats so fast; it could have really helped when he was working.

No more hits. His heart smiled.

A child's protest came from the middle section. "Mommy, I want to go play!" It sounded like Becky, or someone her age. Dimmie didn't dare turn around, risk her seeing him, but his mind checked another box. *I can find a good wife, have a family of my own. I just have to get off the ship. Keep walking.*

When he was only ten feet from the exit, two police officers pushed the door open. Dimmie averted his face as they passed him in the aisle. "What a waste of time," one groused. "The whole ship must have been oblivious. Drunk, most likely. Can you believe we've interviewed half the ship and no one saw anything?"

"Typical," the other agreed. "Maybe Olsen's team ran through the camera feeds by now."

Dimmie quickened his pace. Did the theatre have cameras on the audience? In the dark, during a standing ovation, could one lone man bent over in the back section have been seen? What if the steak knife blade caught the light? A river of sweat ran down his spine.

A jumble of voices in through his mind.

Mam: *You're nothing but a dim wit; you'll never amount to anything.*

Lucky Callahan: *Don't do any thinking. You're no good at it.*

Colin: *You can do anything, my boy, be anything you want.*

Sister Mary Michael: *You're better than you think you are, James-Robert.*

It's now or never, a voice from deep inside added.

I need a crowd.

He and Sean had compared notes last year, after that
bad week when Lucky ordered the hits of three Italians in
one week. A crime spree, the evening news called it. One
station called it an Italian Job, and even Lucky scorned
them for being unoriginal, as if he knew anything about it.
Old man Kerrick had maintained an uneasy truce with the
Italians, so long as they respected the boundaries, but
Lucky got mad like he often did. Something about blocking
his favorite parking place, but the parking spot likely didn't
care about it one way or the other. Sean said he worked
best with a crowd; do the hit, make a noise so people would
come running (they always did) then blend in with the
bystanders. Milling crowds confused the cops, he said, and
with the way people all saw something different, he stood a
good chance of getting away clean.

Dimmie and Sean laughed together, watching the
evening news after one of Sean's hits. The woman with the
flyaway hair and furry microphone interviewed four eye-
witnesses, and every one of them had a different
description of the killers. One said the man was black,
another Asian, the third said it wasn't a man at all, but a
slim woman in a blue dress. So long as none matched
Sean's lanky frame, they could laugh about it over their
black and whites.

That Sean, he sure knew his stuff. Too bad Mr
Kerrick hadn't stayed around to help him, like he was
helping James-Robert. Sean could have been anybody.
Sean was no more. Maybe Dimmie had a bigger obligation
to take Mr Kerrick's help, for Sean's sake.

He squared his shoulders and scanned the theatre. It
looked like one of those anthills he'd seen at home between
the sidewalk cracks; organized, but likely to get off track if
somebody stepped on one ant or dropped a crumb. Several
times, he'd stopped to drip ice cream or drop a crumb of
cookie or bagel, just to watch the ants scurry in different
directions. Nobody else seemed to even see the ants, and
Mam scolded him to step along or she'd whack him a good
one.

Another batch of passengers filed in from the upper
level, streaming in from the corridor behind the maroon
velvet curtains. Crew members directed them to seats,
consulting their clipboards. As far as he could tell, not one
of them was paying any attention to the front of the theatre,
and the newcomers made enough noise to cover his words.

Dimmie walked back to the first row. "All right,
everybody, it's your turn, the first three rows. Hurry along,
now." He stepped aside. Like one of those Thanksgiving
turkey timers, every passenger in the block of seats popped
up and moved into the aisle. James-Robert instructed the
man closest to him, "You, there, go out onto the open deck
and wait for instructions. Don't stop for nothing." He raised
his voice, keeping an eye on the back of the theatre. "The
rest of you, follow him. Let's get this over with."

Without hesitation, the passengers filed down the
aisle, out the door, onto the teak deck and toward the
slanted gangway. He let about forty people pass him. He
noticed a couple of crew members in the back of the theatre
glancing toward the front, and figured it was his time to

leave before they came to see who'd ordered the passengers out of the theatre.

He walked beside the line, keeping his head down; you never knew where cameras might be aimed. It wasn't like the old days, where a man could do whatever he needed to do without his face plastered all over the countryside. He thought of that traffic camera shot of Kerrick. If he'd had a better photo, he would never have hurt that other old man, and he wouldn't be in the fix he was in now.

"Sir?" A woman asked him, "Sir, do you think this will take much longer?" and her friend hushed her. *Marta, don't bother the officer.* Dimmie nodded like any senior staff would and pressed past them. By now, the front of the group was at top of the gangway, unsure if they should head down or wait for further instructions. As Dimmie stepped into the fresh air, a police officer hurried to him. His heart sunk; *so close!*

A new life, a new start, a new Da…stolen from him in the form of a thick Boston accent.

Chapter forty-four

"You, there, you're an officer from the ship, right?" The Boston cop's accent was so strong, it sounded like a cartoon character. "Who said to send the next group out here? We're running a little behind, not ready for them yet. Keep them up here on the deck, all right?" He playfully punched James-Robert's arm. "And thanks for helping us keep the crowd under control. Not what I planned to do on my day off, but you know how that goes, am I right?"

"On the deck?" Dimmie frowned. Not what he needed.

"Yeah, just keep 'em lined up by the railing, outta the rain, will ya, until we can interview them? The boys in the tent are taking their ever-lovin' sweet time about it. Ask 'em, 'did you see anything?' and move them out, that's the way I'd do it, but you know how the brass is." The officer grimaced. "Present company excluded, of course, Sir. I'll be back in a New York minute; gotta check with the bridge, ask 'em about getting a walkie-talkie down here. We're not coordinating with the folks in the theatre. Clearly." He threw a mock salute and headed toward the theatre door.

"Wait." Dimmie strained to keep his face straight as he pulled the white envelope from his breast pocket. "Somebody handed this to me, said to give it to the police commander. You know who he is, right?"

"Big Green Jones? Sure, I know him." The officer turned the envelope in his hand. "I'll see he gets this."

Once the officer was out of sight, Dimmie rehearsed Colin's instructions in his mind. *Walk off the ship like you know where you're going. Stir up a commotion if you have to. Jump in the cab that'll be waiting for you. Go to Quincy Market, blend with the tourists until you're sure no one is following you, then take the T from Haymarket Station to Copley Square and walk across to the Green Tree Hotel. Check in under the name Joseph Horne. It's all arranged. Wait there for me. I'll be there before dinner, aye."*

If there was one thing Dimmie was good at, it was obeying orders.

The group of passengers milled about the deck like a disturbed anthill, and Dimmie knew he'd better take charge before they wandered off or worse. People were like that. *Walk purposefully; talk as if you know of what you speak.* Long-forgotten advice from Sister Mary Michael again; why was she coming to mind now? She was old when Dimmie was in school, likely long gone by now, but he'd take help from any corner. Maybe if she was dead, she had turned into his guardian angel, helping him out when he was in a bind. Did old nun school teachers turn into angels? He'd ask Mr Kerrick about that sometime. They'd have plenty of time to talk, once this was over.

He cleared his throat and barked at the passengers. "All right, now, your attention. Eyes on me. You, there in front, head on down and the rest of you people follow him. Go right into the tent down there. They're waiting for you. Hurry up; you don't want to get wet. The sooner you get interviewed, the sooner you can get back to those drinks with the little paper umbrellas."

The man nearest the gangway moved without hesitation. Several followed, but others murmured. Something about hearing the cop tell them to wait on the deck. Which officer should they listen to?

Dimmie raised his voice, hoping nobody noticed him sweating inside the borrowed jacket. "Move along now, people."

They moved.

The passengers streamed down the gangway, crowding around the two police officers who came out of the tent. The cops waved their clipboards, holding their hands up like crossing guards. A couple of the passengers in front pointed back up the gangway, apparently telling them they'd been sent down to the tent. The officers tried to hold back the milling crowd, but the passengers pressed on, not wanting to be left standing on the slanted gangway, not with the rain picking up.

The commotion outside the tent flaps grew, with passengers pushing to get out of the rain and the police trying to hold them back. James-Robert surveyed the crowd; any minute, somebody was likely to throw a punch, with the way tempers were flaring. You couldn't count on grownups to act like grownups, that's for sure. As many buckets of beer he'd seen on the ship, this bunch might be even less predictable than most.

He glanced toward the fence butting against the terminal building. The gate was closed, but he couldn't be sure if it was locked until he tested it. Tuesday, when the

Ocean Serenity was actually due to port in Boston, the parking lot would bulge with buses and cabs and people waving signs for tours. Today, the port was closed except for the investigation. Beyond the deserted parking lot, traffic surged like any other day in any major city, people ignoring the drama playing out. One young lone woman behind the fence bent over a stroller, probably telling her child about the big boat. Why did mothers take their babies out in the rain, even with that plastic awning on the stroller? When he had a child of his own, he'd keep her safe and dry.

He measured the fence with his eyes. Even if he had to scale it, if the gate didn't open, he could be over it in no time. He'd outrun enough cops in his life, and what was a measly chain-link fence? It wasn't even loose, like so many fences in the city. Sagging fences were harder to climb. This fence would be a piece of cake, not like last month over on 16th street, the one with the rottweilers. Talk about a junkyard dog. Spotting a lone green cab idling near the fence, Dimmie's upper lip twitched. Colin had called for it, like he said he would. All he had to do was reach that cab.

Nothing would stop him now.

He strode the final few yards down the Promenade deck and edged between the last handful of passengers walking down the gangway. He was careful to not touch the rope handrail; Colin said that would be a giveaway, if anyone was looking. As often as officers clambered up and down those gangways, they didn't need to hang onto the rope railings like those unsteady passengers. *Keep your fingerprints on your hands,* Brody always said, not wanting to leave any trace evidence for cops to pick up.

Brody: he'd forgotten about Brody. Poor guy would hear all about it when Dimmie didn't show up at the Greyhound station. Good thing Brody knew how to duck whatever Lucky Callahan threw. Lucky would be in rare form once he found out Dimmie wasn't coming back no more. Well, he wouldn't be there to take the flak, and soon as the cops read that letter he'd written, Lucky wouldn't be there for long, either.

Back in his suite, Colin had assured James-Robert he could manage each step of the plan. *One foot in front of the other,* he said, although Dimmie didn't know any other way to walk. He knew about cabs; he took them at home, sometimes, when he had money to spare. Mostly he walked. He liked the energy of the city.

The T sounded funny, but Colin told him it was just like the subways in the city, except the stations were taller and maybe it smelled a little better. More modern. Boston's city council didn't smile on street performers, either, so maybe there wouldn't be any buskers in the station. Dimmie memorized Colin's directions to the T: go behind Quincy Market to the intersection of Congress and New Sudbury, find the sign for Haymarket Station, buy your ticket from the machine, and get on the Orange Line.

"Those words sound funny to me. And why is it a color instead of a number, like in the city?"

Colin chuckled. "You have no idea how many funny names there are in this country, my boy. So many towns are named for Indian words, Spanish words, French even, all part of the melting pot that makes this country great. You've lived in the city your whole life, and that's a good thing, but a better thing is to get out and see what the Good Lord put there for us to enjoy. Every place is different, you'll see."

Dimmie ventured, "Can we go see some of those places I read about in my books, do you think? Maybe even the Grand Canyon or Yellowstone?"

"Count on it, my boy, but first things first. Get off the T at Copley Square and …"

Chapter forty-five

A crowd.

Dimmie needed an unruly crowd, and these calm cruise passengers weren't cutting it. He drew a deep breath and shoved the man in front of him. Flailing his arms, the man stumbled into the woman ahead of him on the ramp and six more passengers went down like those dominoes the kids played with in Central Park, only dominoes were quiet and these passengers raised a ruckus. The man caught himself with the rope rail and turned to take a swing at whoever pushed him. In the crush, it could have been anybody. Quick on his feet, Dimmie leaped over the railing on the gangway, dropping half a dozen feet to the concrete pier. He landed lightly — not his first time — and shoved the back of another young man, plowing him into the crowd. The guy grabbed a woman's large purse to stop his fall and she screamed, "Stop, thief!" Angry voices shouted, she swung her purse at his head, and the cops finally looked up from their clipboards.

Dimmie slowed behind a woman with a large hat, as innocent as the day he was born, unbuttoning his jacket. The police scanned the packed crowd, looking for the cause of the uproar. Unable to see the perpetrators, they grabbed a few of the closest passengers by the arms and ordered the others to stop. One yelled into the transmitter on his shoulder.

Dimmie didn't have much time. Cops everywhere were good at restoring order; they were trained in that. Their training didn't extend to shooting. He'd seen off-duty cops at the shooting range, and they were the most erratic shooters there. Aim? They shot like they had their eyes closed, missing the whole target half the time. Brody warned Dimmie not to shoot like he usually did when cops were at the range. Miss a few targets until they left so they wouldn't be suspicious.

Several passengers shouted, "I didn't do anything wrong! Take your hands of me! Police brutality!" like they do on the news. The police officers' faces were set, slapping handcuffs on people, lining them up against the side of the tent. Police did that; if they didn't know who to talk to, they stopped everybody. Like Mr Andy said, sort 'em out later.

Ducking behind one of those tall A-frame signs — this one advertising a New! Great! Fresh! Seafood! restaurant — he slipped off the Second Officer's jacket and dropped it into a covered trash bin. In navy tee shirt and black trousers, he eased his way back between the passengers. Those in the rear hadn't seen who triggered the skirmish and didn't spare him a second glance. Fists were flying by the tent, but Dimmie didn't have time to enjoy the show.

He edged his way to the far side of the crowd, toward the line of yellow Caution tape the police had strung up. He liked to stop and watch the police work inside that tape at home, but he didn't have time to admire their skills today. They had their hands full with more people than they could handle, the rain was picking up, and with tempers heating up, nobody gave him a second glance.

Keeping an eye on the nearest officer, he ducked under the Caution tape and walked *boldly, briskly,* toward the terminal. A few feet from the glass doors, Dimmie sidestepped and touched the gate. It gave under his pressure, swung wide open. Stupid cops; did they think they could control over two thousand cruise passengers with a tent and bit of yellow plastic tape? Well, they had, until he stirred things up.

Dimmie pulled the chain-link gate closed behind him and jogged the few yards to the waiting green cab. The driver saw him coming and held open the door for him.

Dimmie slid into the back seat. "Quincy Market, and step on it."

As the driver pulled into traffic, Dimmie looked over his shoulder. The skirmish by the police tent was settling down, from what he could tell. Up on one of the white balconies, two decks down from the top of the ship, stood a lone man with a suitcase by his feet. Colin Kerrick raised one arm in a wave, doffing his fedora with the other hand.

"What's your hurry? Somebody after you or what?" The cabbie smiled in the mirror. "Catch your breath. I tell you, a day like this makes a person happy to be alive."

Dimmie settled back into his seat. "You have no idea, man."

If you enjoyed The Dim-Witted Hitman, please take a moment to post a positive review. They mean more than you know, and Dimmie's going to need all the help he can get.

Excerpt from **Murder on Deck**

by Deb Graham

What am I doing on another cruise? I could have talked them into a nice, safe camping trip instead. I should have taken up Nan's invitation to visit them on Kauai. I should have–

Fingering her new necklace, Jerria stood on the balcony of the *Ocean Journey,* watching the frenzied pace below. On the pier, forklifts shuttled pallets and crates of foodstuffs and other supplies to the waiting ship, while a stream of passengers made their way up the inclined gangway. The California sunshine warmed her face, but failed to touch the chill in her heart.

She mentally scolded herself, rubbing her arms. *Knock it off. The chances of another major crime on a cruise ship are as remote as Will ordering salad for lunch. Nothing's going to happen. I love Alaska, so what am I worried about?*

Will called from the stateroom. "What's taking so long?"

She squared her shoulders and stepped through the open doorway. *Nothing's going to happen; I'll enjoy this cruise like everybody else.* It wasn't her fault, after all, that trouble seemed to follow her.

By the time they'd climbed the four flights to the upper deck, the sleet had turned to thin rain. They staked out a spot under an overhang. Ahead lay the Hubbard Glacier's face, and dozens of passengers gathered to be the first to see it. More stood in the observation lounge, protected from the elements.

The *Ocean Journey* slowed, gliding through the inky water, tall cliffs rising on port and starboard as the bay narrowed. Its engines only a low hum, the silence of the bay pressed in on the ship. Crew members offered plaid wool blankets. Nan gratefully wrapped two around herself, while Jerria and Charlie took one each. Will zipped his waterproof jacket.

Jerria surveyed nearby passengers arrayed in Alaska-emblemed ponchos, jackets, sweatshirts, even suspenders, and chuckled. "They'll look silly wearing that stuff at home, but at least they're warm."

She heard a scuffle and a thump across the deck. Heads swiveled. A man lay on the deck, his nose bleeding, unmoving.

"We were just standing here, and he fell over!" a woman cried. "He's not going to die, is he? Help, somebody!" Two passengers and a crew member ran to his side.

A medical team quickly removed the fallen man, and passengers turned their attention back to the scenery. As the ship gradually eased up the fjord, ice from the distant glacier bobbed in the water below, thicker than earlier, bumping against the hull of the ship. Someone joked about the *Titanic*. No one laughed.

Joel stood a few feet away, binoculars in hand. "We may not make it all the way to the glacier's face. Captain McCann's very cautious of the ice, but we're going as far as we can go safely. Hubbard Glacier is about seventy-six miles long. Did you all see the colors of the bergies? You can see how much ice is underwater compared to above the surface. It's the same with the glacier itself. Nearly two hundred eighty feet of ice is under the water and..."

Three moose and a calf nibbled bushes on the shore, silently watching the ship glide past, unconcerned. A while later, three white-jacketed crew members circled through the passengers with trays of steaming mugs. "Hot soup, anyone? Beef barley soup here."

Most passengers accepted the mugs, cradling them in their hands, soaking in the warmth. A woman shied away, insisting, "How can you trust food, when so many people are sick? I'm not eating another thing until I'm back in civilization!"

A nearby passenger snorted. "Some people need an excuse to lose some weight. Take any incentive you can get, lady. You look like a walrus in that coat."

"How dare you! I paid good money for this new coat, I'll have you know. I certainly don't need to lose weight, you big oaf!"

"Hey, no skin off my nose, if you're one of those people who can't see what's in the mirror. You aren't even smart enough to know boiling soup kills germs."

"Well, I *never!*" She took a swing at him, sputtering. The man ducked. Swiftly, her partner grabbed her arm.

"Come on, let's go on the other side, away from him. We don't need to be around stupid people. Obviously, he doesn't know a thing about fashion."

Her face flushed, the woman stalked across the deck to the far railing.

Joel raised his voice, his eyes flickering back and forth. "Look, there's an otter on that bergie, holding its favorite rock. Every day, they choose a rock and carry it with them. It comes in handy for opening clams and other snacks. Keep an eye out for seals, too. They look like floating logs at first, until you make out their faces."

Jerria shook her head. "Tension's rising. I hope they get a handle on this soon."

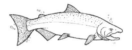

Captain McCann's voice came over the loudspeaker, muffled by the surrounding cliffs. "Good news, on two fronts. First, you'll be glad to know the CDC folks agree we can revoke the red alert status in the galley. That means our talented chefs will be serving a full menu, starting with dinner this evening." She chuckled. "I expected that; I can hear your cheer even up here in the bridge. Second, due to our schedule change, we're in no rush to leave Hubbard Glacier today, as long as we're out of the harbor by dusk. So relax, take in the beauty, and enjoy the day, folks."

A man nearby sighed. "All we have is time."

"Time, and a decent dinner tonight," Will grinned. "In danger of losing weight myself."

As the ship gently rounded the bend, Hubbard Glacier's face came into view just as the sun broke through the clouds. Even from a distance, its vivid colors rising three hundred fifty feet above the water caused a collective gasp. Captain McCann eased the ship closer.

"I didn't know glaciers have a voice. No wonder the early people believe they're alive. With all that creaking and groaning, I feel its spirit." Nan stared. "That huge piece to the left is definitely leaning. Do you think it'll calve while we're watching?"

"Sometimes they hang like that for a long time, so there's no way of knowing," Jerria replied. "There it goes...oh!" An iceberg the size of a ranch house sheared off, crashing into the sea. A wave crested with ice splashed over floating floes. Two sea lions tipped into the water. Passengers clapped.

"I saw a documentary, where people actually surf on the waves made by glaciers calving. I love to surf, but that's plain foolhardy." Charlie pointed to the water. "Look, there goes a lifeboat."

One of the small boats from the *Ocean Journey* skimmed across the bay, dwarfed by the massive glacier. Two orange-overalled crew members dodged iceberg bits, guiding the boat closer to the glacier face. Another ice shelf calved free, sliding into the sea, triggering a tall wave that raced swiftly toward the lifeboat. Jerria's heart skipped a beat, watching anxiously with others lining the rail. The crewmembers frantically turned the boat's bow into the oncoming wave, riding the crest like a roller coaster. Passengers breathed a collective sigh of relief.

Danger passed –for now- Jerria watched a man in the boat lean over the side. Using ice clamps, he and his partner wrestled a chunk of ice into the lifeboat, waved, then maneuvered the little boat back toward the ship. On the port side, a davit lowered into the water. The boat rose, crew, ice, and all, to the Promenade deck. A few minutes later, they came onto the upper deck, pushing a cart with the ice chunk they'd retrieved on it.

Joel pulled the cart to the open deck. "There you are. I was afraid that wave would swamp you guys. This piece is a beauty. Come closer, everybody. The older, denser ice is the deeper blue and... Oh, no, you don't!"

Joel stepped in front of the glacial ice, his arms spread protectively. He glared at the two white-aproned crew members bearing ice carving tools. "No. Way. This ice was probably fluffy snow about the time of the Crusades. You two are *not* turning it into a race car or dragon!"

Taking one look at Joel's face, the ice carvers retreated into the ship.

Nan shivered as the afternoon progressed. "That breeze feels like somebody left the freezer door open. But I'm enjoying this so much! Oh, I think it's going to calve again."

After the berg broke free, the four friends retreated to the lounge, where they could watch the scenery behind glass. The ship gradually backed out of the narrow fjord, toward open sea. A waiter offered mugs of hot chocolate.

Nan cradled her mug in her icy fingers. "You were right; I'm never going to forget this!"

"It's been a gorgeous day," Jerria agreed. "I keep thinking about Elias and Penny. They would have loved to see the glacier. I wonder how Penny is getting on."

Nan loosened her wooly scarf. "All she can do is go on living until she feels alive again. I thought the illness had run its course, but then that man collapsed on deck earlier..."

"Oh, no, you don't," Will's eyes twinkled. "Can't go worrying. Come on, time for a game of shuffleboard before dinner. Men against the women, and losers buy dinner in the dining room."

Jerria stood. "You're on! But dinner? That's already paid for. How about you and Charlie bring me and Nan hot fudge sundaes before bed, since we're going to win?"

"Maybe skip the ice cream and just bring me a bowl of hot fudge. I don't think I'll ever be warm again." Nan sighed. "The ship doesn't have an *indoor* shuffleboard court, does it?"

As they waited for the aft elevator, Jerria overheard a woman comforting a girl in the nearby stairwell.

"Don't cry. I agree, it's not right, and I know you played your best, but it's just a game."

"But, Mom, we *won!* Liza gave the second-place team cool water bottles, and gave us *stickers*! She said we weren't old enough for water bottles, but it's not like they had beer or something in them. It's not *fair!*"

As the elevator door closed, the girl's last words carried plainly. "I'm never going on another stupid cruise in my whole life, and you can't make me."

Captain McCann's voice came over the loudspeaker, muffled by the surrounding cliffs. "Good news, on two fronts. First, you'll be glad to know the CDC folks agree we can revoke the red alert status in the galley. That means our talented chefs will be serving a full menu, starting with dinner this evening." She chuckled. "I expected that; I can hear your cheer even up here in the bridge. Second, due to our schedule change, we're in no rush to leave Hubbard Glacier today, as long as we're out of the harbor by dusk. So relax, take in the beauty, and enjoy the day, folks."

A man nearby sighed. "All we have is time."

"Time, and a decent dinner tonight," Will grinned. "In danger of losing weight myself."

As the ship gently rounded the bend, Hubbard Glacier's face came into view just as the sun broke through the clouds. Even from a distance, its vivid colors rising three hundred fifty feet above the water caused a collective gasp. Captain McCann eased the ship closer.

"I didn't know glaciers have a voice. No wonder the early people believe they're alive. With all that creaking and groaning, I feel its spirit." Nan stared. "That huge piece to the left is definitely leaning. Do you think it'll calve while we're watching?"

"Sometimes they hang like that for a long time, so there's no way of knowing," Jerria replied. "There it goes...oh!" An iceberg the size of a ranch house sheared off, crashing into the sea. A wave crested with ice splashed over floating floes. Two sea lions tipped into the water. Passengers clapped.

"I saw a documentary, where people actually surf on the waves made by glaciers calving. I love to surf, but that's plain foolhardy." Charlie pointed to the water. "Look, there goes a lifeboat."

One of the small boats from the *Ocean Journey* skimmed across the bay, dwarfed by the massive glacier. Two orange-overalled crew members dodged iceberg bits, guiding the boat closer to the glacier face. Another ice shelf calved free, sliding into the sea, triggering a tall wave that raced swiftly toward the lifeboat. Jerria's heart skipped a beat, watching anxiously with others lining the rail. The crewmembers frantically turned the boat's bow into the oncoming wave, riding the crest like a roller coaster. Passengers breathed a collective sigh of relief.

Danger passed –for now– Jerria watched a man in the boat lean over the side. Using ice clamps, he and his partner wrestled a chunk of ice into the lifeboat, waved, then maneuvered the little boat back toward the ship. On the port side, a davit lowered into the water. The boat rose, crew, ice, and all, to the Promenade deck. A few minutes later, they came onto the upper deck, pushing a cart with the ice chunk they'd retrieved on it.

Joel pulled the cart to the open deck. "There you are. I was afraid that wave would swamp you guys. This piece is a beauty. Come closer, everybody. The older, denser ice is the deeper blue and... Oh, no, you don't!"

Joel stepped in front of the glacial ice, his arms spread protectively. He glared at the two white-aproned crew members bearing ice carving tools. "No. Way. This ice was probably fluffy snow about the time of the Crusades. You two are *not* turning it into a race car or dragon!"

Taking one look at Joel's face, the ice carvers retreated into the ship.

Nan shivered as the afternoon progressed. "That breeze feels like somebody left the freezer door open. But I'm enjoying this so much! Oh, I think it's going to calve again."

After the berg broke free, the four friends retreated to the lounge, where they could watch the scenery behind glass. The ship gradually backed out of the narrow fjord, toward open sea. A waiter offered mugs of hot chocolate.

Nan cradled her mug in her icy fingers. "You were right; I'm never going to forget this!"

"It's been a gorgeous day," Jerria agreed. "I keep thinking about Elias and Penny. They would have loved to see the glacier. I wonder how Penny is getting on."

Nan loosened her wooly scarf. "All she can do is go on living until she feels alive again. I thought the illness had run its course, but then that man collapsed on deck earlier..."

"Oh, no, you don't," Will's eyes twinkled. "Can't go worrying. Come on, time for a game of shuffleboard before dinner. Men against the women, and losers buy dinner in the dining room."

Jerria stood. "You're on! But dinner? That's already paid for. How about you and Charlie bring me and Nan hot fudge sundaes before bed, since we're going to win?"

"Maybe skip the ice cream and just bring me a bowl of hot fudge. I don't think I'll ever be warm again." Nan sighed. "The ship doesn't have an *indoor* shuffleboard court, does it?"

As they waited for the aft elevator, Jerria overheard a woman comforting a girl in the nearby stairwell.

"Don't cry. I agree, it's not right, and I know you played your best, but it's just a game."

"But, Mom, we *won!* Liza gave the second-place team cool water bottles, and gave us *stickers*! She said we weren't old enough for water bottles, but it's not like they had beer or something in them. It's not *fair*!"

As the elevator door closed, the girl's last words carried plainly. "I'm never going on another stupid cruise in my whole life, and you can't make me."

Come along on an Alaskan cruise with Jerria and Will, with ports so vivid, you could plan your own cruise. Minus the poison, of course. Read **Murder on Deck**.

Other Books by Deb Graham

The Cookie Cutter Legacy

Murder on Deck   *a cruise novel*

Peril In Paradise   *a cruise novel*

Tips From The Cruise Addict's Wife

More Tips From The Cruise Addict's Wife

Mediterranean Cruise With The Cruise Addict's Wife

Alaskan Cruise by the Cruise Addict's Wife

Hand Me That Hand Pie!

Busy Kids, Happy Kids

How To Write Your Story

How To Complain...and get what you deserve

Hungry Kids Campfire Cookbook

Kid Food On A Stick

Quick and Clever Kids' Crafts

Awesome Science Experiments for Kids

Made in the USA
Las Vegas, NV
25 April 2021

22004914R00135